THE QUEEN'S HANDBOOK

TO ESSENCE AND EMBERS

(Book 3 in the Stolen Spells series)

by

Tish Thawer

www.amberleafpublishing.com
www.tishthawer.com

The Queen's Handbook to Essence and Embers Copyright© 2024 by Tish Thawer. All rights reserved.

No part of this book may be used or reproduced in any manner whatsoever, including Internet usage, without written permission from Amber Leaf Publishing, except in the case of brief quotations embodied in articles and reviews.

First Edition
First Hardback Printing, 2024
ISBN: 979-8-3302-8923-3

Cover design by Molly Phipps of We Got You Covered Book Design
Edited by Ang'dora Productions
Character Illustration by Cameo.Draws

This book is a work of fiction. All characters, names, places, organizations, events and incidents portrayed in this novel are either products of the author's imagination or are used fictitiously. Any resemblance to actual persons, living or dead, events or establishments is solely coincidental or used herein under the Fair Use Act.

Amber Leaf Publishing, Missouri
www.amberleafpublishing.com
www.tishthawer.com

Praise for *The Witch Handbook to Magic and Mayhem*

"No one writes magic like Tish Thawer! What a wonderful, heart-wrenching adventure she penned in *The Witch Handbook to Magic and Mayhem*!"
~ **Casey L. Bond, author of *Where Oceans Burn***

"Tish Thawer has me under her spell once more! With stunning imagery, engaging characters, and an intriguing plot that will have you on the edge of your seat, *The Witch Handbook to Magic and Mayhem* should be on your must-read list for 2023!"
~ **Stacey Rourke, Award-winning Author**

"Whimsy and worry make this an exhilarating ride. Thawer has created another mesmerizing world where the good guys and bad guys may not be exactly what they seem, and the twists and turns keep you wanting more."
~ **Brynn Myers, Paranormal Romance Author**

"There aren't enough words to describe how much I love this story. The sisters are fantastic. The story is simply just magical. With plenty of twists and turns, this story is one that you will not want to put down."
~ **Goodreads Reviewer**

Praise for *Weaver*

"Visually stunning, Thawer's *Weaver* is a fresh YA Fantasy that will capture your heart and convince your mind dreams really do come true."
~ Stacey Rourke, Award-winning Author

"Atmospheric. Magical. And swoon worthy. Thawer's YA Fantasy is full of *Practical Magic* vibes and will have you rushing to bed in search of a Weaver of your own."
~ Belinda Boring, International Bestselling Author

"Lush and atmospheric, *Weaver* is a beautiful, carefully-crafted YA fantasy."
~ Casey L. Bond, Author of *House of Eclipses*

"An illustrious YA Fantasy that blurs the line between dreams and reality, obscuring together two worlds into one visionary romance."
~ Cambria Hebert, Award-winning Author

"A beautifully written YA fantasy, wrapped in darkness and love. *Weaver* is full of stunning imagery and unforgettable characters that will keep you turning the pages until morning."
~ Rebecca L. Garcia, Author of *Shadow Kissed*

"Spellbinding and packed with mystery and breathtaking landscapes, the world of the Weaver will assuredly enchant you."
~ Cameo Renae, USA Today Bestselling Author

Praise for *The Witches of BlackBrook*

"Tish Thawer's intriguing story line is weaved and crafted into a magical and spellbinding web that kept me up until the wee hours of the morning biting my finger nails and cheering for the sisters. Strong story line and well-developed characters that will sweep you away. I was completely floored by this amazing book and I recommend it to everyone!"
~ Voluptuous Book Diva

"Tish Thawer is an amazing wordsmith. I have devoured several books by her and she never disappoints. The blend of history with contemporary is just genius and I can't wait to see what this author will come up with next. Add this to your list as a must-read recommendation from me! An EASY 5 out of 5 stars!"
~ NerdGirl Melanie

"Overall, The Witches of BlackBrook was a grand slam for me. I was so enchanted by this spellbinding tale of hope, love, and a bond that can't be broken. There was something special about it and I honestly think it had something for all different types of readers. Whether you're into romance, historical, paranormal, new adult, etc. the author effortlessly weaves so many elements together to create a flawless experience for whoever picks it up. If you're looking to be enchanted and escape your mind for a couple hours, I highly suggest picking up The Witches of BlackBrook and diving on in!!"
~ Candy of Prisoners of Print

"From essence to embers, and embers to dust. A Queen will always do as she must!"

~ Tish Thawer

I
Essence

One

Ferindale - Present Day

Lily

Flames licked the treetops, singeing their pink petals black as I strained to control my elemental power.

"Goodness gracious, Lily! You're going to burn down the whole damn castle!" Aster's panicked response was one of many I'd heard over the last hour and a half.

"I'm sorry. I really *am* trying my best." Gaining control over the element I shared with Alder was paramount, but despite my efforts I continued to struggle. And it seemed Daisy did, too.

Blowing uncontrolled through the trees, Daisy's wind whipped the flames into a frenzy, snapping branches and raining charred limbs down upon our heads.

"Look out!" she screamed.

Thankfully, Fern and Iris were there.

With a twist of their wrists, the twins worked in unison to douse the flames, sparing us from the burning foliage thanks to Fern's water magic and Iris's earth affinity.

"Wow! You two are getting good." I beamed.

Fully recovered after the crone was destroyed, Iris and Fern's twin bond had returned. And with their fae powers released, both seemed to be thriving here in the fairy realm—in *my* realm.

My heart raced at the thought.

Having my family here, in our united kingdom, was a dream come true—one I never thought possible. But after moving back to the Dark castle in Dartmoor, Alder and I relinquished the Light castle to my sisters who stayed in Ferindale and made it their home. Mom, Sybil, and Aster remained through the winter, helping them to settle in, but when spring broke, our mother and the leader of the Acrucian Coven returned to our original world to attend to their duties there, while we continued to understand our new roles here. We all missed Mom every day, but with the hidden portal in the basement of our old home now secure, she could return at any time. Unfortunately, her visits were happening less and less. I think she still struggled to be here with Gideon gone, but it was a subject none of us had the heart to broach with her just yet.

The years the Dark King spent in our world and the bargain he made to keep me safe hinged on his and my mother's relationship. But after witnessing her reaction to his death, I knew there was more to it than that. I think she loved Gideon, and I hoped with time, her heart would begin to heal from his loss.

"Try again." Aster's brisk command pulled me from my thoughts.

I turned back to the target and let the warmth of my elemental gift flow through my veins. Before all of our powers were released, I only used Alder's gift to stay warm, barely testing its limits the few times I felt brave. Since then, each of my sisters received an elemental gift of their own, and we began to train together: earth, air, fire, and water. We'd all been able to produce traces of our element and manipulate them to our will—some better than others.

It was no surprise Fern received the water element to compliment her flower and herb magic, while Iris received earth, which related directly to her crystals and their grounding energy. Daisy's air element was the perfect complement for her apothecary skills in healing the body and mind. And me, with my candlelight and revelation magic, fire seemed the obvious choice, despite my lack of control just yet.

I glanced at Daisy, whose hesitant expression knotted my gut. I was unsure why she and I still struggled so much, but until we figured it out, Aster had tasked us to practice every day in the back garden of the Ferindale castle.

"Come on, Lil. Don't be afraid. You can't get better if you're scared of your gift."

I cocked my head. "I'm not scared, Aster. I'm simply trying to identify what's wrong."

"Don't."

"Don't what?" I asked, confused.

"Don't try to figure out what's wrong." She took two steps in my direction, then stopped and tapped a finger to her temple. "You're too much in your head. You simply have to let it flow, like the rest of your magic."

Her words struck hard. Not from harshness, or embarrassment on my part, but because they were true. We'd all grown up as witches in a house full of magic and a shop that literally used fae magic to exist on our plane. Utilizing this new element should be no different. I simply needed to relax.

I closed my eyes and reached for the flames again. Like warm honey, the element flowed through me, mixing with the electrical energy of my fae and witch magic that had been a part of me since I was born. Opening my eyes, I held out my arm and imagined a small ball of fire, then smiled when it sparked to life in the palm of my hand.

"There. Good. Now hold it steady," Aster coached.

Gazing into the dancing flames, I welcomed the feel of it against my skin. Warm but not harmful, it radiated through my body and deep into my soul. I closed my eyes and concentrated on the moment. I wanted to remember what it felt like—*needed* to remember it if I was going to master its energy and produce flames on a whim.

My eyes snapped open when the flaming ball sputtered in my palm, turning from a golden orange to a hot, vibrant blue. Sparks snapped and spit from its edge, dropping tiny balls of fire onto the ground and igniting the moss on which I stood.

Fern quickly doused them again.

"Dammit!" I stomped from the smoldering greenery and collapsed onto a stone bench in defeat. "I don't understand what's wrong. I'm the Fae Queen, the most powerful of us all. This should be easy for me!" I looked up at my sisters and apologized immediately. "I'm sorry. I didn't mean any offense. I just expected as the only *full* fae here, I would be able to gain control with ease, and it's frustrating that I can't." I lowered my head, noting tiny blue flowers sprouting around my boots.

"Sorrow and guilt," Fern whispered on a delicate breath.

"What?" I asked.

"The flowers blooming beneath your feet. They represent sorrow and guilt. It may be what's blocking you." She met my eyes with a sympathetic gaze.

Staring at the small star-shaped petals, I lost myself to her words. After learning the truth of who I was, I'd been thrust into this realm and into this unexpected life where we had all experienced sorrow and loss, but none more than Alder.

An image of my beautiful husband formed in my mind.

He had lost his mother, his childhood, and his father—all at the hands of my biological dad. The Light King, Thadius, was a son of a bitch, and I certainly didn't feel guilty he was gone. On the other hand, an image of Gideon blossomed next to Alder, and I realized where my guilt must lie.

"I think that's enough for today," Aster announced. "Let's all get some rest, and we'll meet back here tomorrow morning. Sound good?"

Replies of acknowledgment and acceptance sounded from my sisters, while I remained seated on the cold stone bench. "Sounds good," I lied.

Two

Lily

"Did you want to be alone?" Daisy shuffled in my direction, snuffing out any remaining embers with the tip of her black boot.

"Yes... No. I'm not sure." I shrugged, feeling like the lost little sister once again. With my true identity revealed, I was the oldest among us all, but growing up the baby of the family—as fake as that may have been—in times like this, it still felt real to me.

"If it helps, I don't understand what my problem is either." Daisy joined me on the bench as the others returned inside. Her gaze narrowed on their backs as she watched the castle door close behind them. "Have you had any other visions?" she whispered, bringing to light the shared secret we'd been carrying for weeks.

I lowered my head. "No. Just the one."

"Me, either, thank the Goddess."

Thank the Goddess. Unfortunately, I believed *another* Goddess was responsible for our current issues. One with malicious intent.

Three months ago, just before my move to Dartmoor, Daisy and I awoke in a fright, our mental bond confirming the same dark vision had plagued both our dreams. After speaking to our sisters the following morning, we quickly realized it had only affected the two of us. Dark energy spewed from a crack in the ground, creeping like vines over the manicured gardens of the Dartmoor castle, creating a common concern for us both—that Macha's influence may have not fully left Daisy after all.

Macha was a dark witch and the Fae Goddess of Death the crone called on for her spells. *And* the Goddess Daisy had called on when she was trying to save me. We assumed the dark witch's influence had seeped into my psyche while I was connected to Daisy, unlocking her fae powers, but until we learned the truth, it was a secret we shared and both agreed to keep.

"Do you think we should tell Aster?" Daisy's voice remained a whisper on the wind.

After everything that happened with Fern and me recently, Daisy and Aster weren't exactly seeing eye-to-eye. But if it meant helping me and the rest of our family, she would serve herself up for more of Aster's disappointment. It's just who she was.

"No. Until we have a firm answer, we keep the vision to ourselves." I refused to let the bravest of us be blamed for her selfless actions again.

Daisy nodded, her shoulders sinking with relief as she changed the subject. "How are you and Alder liking the Dark castle?"

I dipped my head and smiled. Despite us dissolving the concept of the Light and Dark courts, we still couldn't help ourselves when referencing the realms. It proved a hard habit to break. But even with its original designation, our *dark* home felt as light as could be. "It's fantastic. We're very happy there and have been enjoying making the castle our own."

An image of Alder's face formed in my mind, his gorgeous features hovering over me as we made love in the dining room beneath the high glass ceiling. The memory of his regal antlers and broad shoulders melding with the stars of the night sky brought a blush to my cheeks. There were times I could still hardly believe this was my life, but now I knew it was one I'd never give up.

The pain of Gideon's loss continued to haunt the halls and our hearts, but Alder and I vowed to make new memories together, knowing it's what he would have wanted us to do. As the previous Dark King, Gideon spent most of his life in my world, protecting me, so re-building a relationship with his son after being separated for so long was a short-lived dream that Alder still mourned. Despite his dark title and everlasting presence, Gideon was the kindest, most self-sacrificing of us all. He would not be forgotten.

Daisy caught my eye and smiled. "Bennett and I are doing well, too." Her cheeks flushed red.

After they'd fallen for each other during our recent adventure, I told them I was happy for them both, and I was. Once Bennett had revealed his true self and explained the situation of how he was forced to steal the crone's book to garner favor for his clan and save his mother's life, he had truly proven himself again while attempting to save me in the Dark Elf stronghold. That, in and of itself, made it far easier for Alder and me to forgive him. Now we were thrilled he chose to stay on as a guard in our army and explore what he and Daisy had started together. Daisy, of course, was happiest of all.

Their mutual respect and concern for our family had turned into long walks and heartfelt talks as they strolled around Ferindale, getting to know one another. Now, whenever he wasn't training with the Guard—or she with us in the garden—the two of them were inseparable.

"Speak of the devil." I lifted my chin.

Daisy beamed as Bennett emerged from the castle door and headed in our direction.

"Hello. Am I interrupting? I saw the rest of your sisters inside and got concerned." Bennett ran a hand through his platinum blond hair, which was still a strange sight to see.

He was no longer the nerdy plant-boy I knew back in Essex, hiding behind his shadow magic glamor. Now, his true self—a fae warrior and witch in our royal army—stood before me, and I was elated I could once again call him my friend.

"We're fine." Daisy rose from the bench and up on to her toes to press a quick peck to his cheek. "But thank you for coming to check on us."

Bennett smiled in awe as he looked at Daisy, then bowed in respect as he turned to me. "Your Majesty, I believe your husband was looking for you as well."

Your Majesty. That was another thing I was still working on getting used to.

"Thank you." I rose from the bench. "I'll see you both tomorrow." I hugged Daisy and whispered in her ear, "I'll see if I can recreate the vision tonight to gain some insight."

My youngest sister pulled back with panic in her eyes and replied with only one word before I walked away.

"Don't."

Three

Alder

"Hello, my darling." I greeted my wife as soon as I stepped through the castle's back door. "I was just coming to find you."

"So Bennett said. Are you ready to go home?"

"Yes. We had a long training day, and I'm ready to relax with my beautiful queen." I bent down and placed my lips against hers. A thin layer of dried sweat remained on my skin, giving our kiss a slightly salty taste, but she didn't seem to mind.

"Seems I could use a bath," I admitted.

Lily wrapped her arms around my waist and pushed her chest against me. "I like where this is headed."

I closed my eyes and reveled in her soft, joyful laugh as I reached into my pocket and tossed a portal ball onto the ground. "Me too."

Moments later, we stepped through the portal, returning to the dining hall of our Dark castle in Dartmoor.

"Home sweet home." I took Lily's hand and led her from the glass-topped room, pausing only to notify the staff we'd return in an hour for dinner. "So, how did your training go today?" I asked as soon as we were alone.

"Same as before. Terrible." She hung her head and stared at the onyx steps as we climbed our way to the bedroom hall.

"Do you still think it has something to do with Daisy's connection to Macha?"

Lily may have kept the secret from her sisters but said she refused to hide anything from me.

"Yes. Unfortunately. But I was thinking of doing some dreamwork tonight to see if I could gain more insight to their connection." She paused outside of our bedroom door. "But that means we'll have to sleep apart. Are you okay with that?" She glanced up at me with her beautiful green eyes, most likely noting the dark swirl that appeared in mine whenever I became worried or upset. "We can have Gretta set up the couch in our room, if you'd prefer," she added in a rush.

I squeezed her hand, my concern easing a fraction. "Okay, yes. I can work with that."

As if by magic, Gretta appeared at the end of the hall just as we entered our room.

"Did I hear my name?" she asked and followed us inside.

"Yes. Could you please bring up the bedding and dress the couch for tonight?" Lily nodded to the oversized, chocolate brown velvet sofa that sat on the far side of the room.

Gretta turned to me with a glint in her eye. "Is someone in the doghouse?" she teased.

I may be her king, but I was also her friend—and the boy she'd taken care of since the day I was born, despite us looking almost the same age.

I chuckled and shook my head. "No, nothing like that." I pulled Lily into my arms and ran a hand down her silken red hair. "My wife will be doing some dreamwork tonight and doesn't want to *injure* me in the process."

Gretta stiffened, her focus snapping to Lily. "Magic… while you sleep? Are you sure that's safe?"

Lily lifted her chin. "Most of the time, yes. But that's why we're prepping the couch. Just in case. That way Alder can wake me if anything seems amiss."

Gretta's eyes may not darken like mine, but it was clear she was unsure of Lily's plan as well. She moved with an uncharacteristic stiffness to her actions, retrieving the bedding and snapping the sheets fiercely before tucking them beneath the cushions with sharp, precise jabs. "All done."

"Thank you," Lily offered hesitantly.

Gretta looked to me. "With your permission, I'd like to stay in the room across the hall tonight… to remain close in case you need anything."

I took a deep breath, my chest slowly rising and falling, and held my response for an extra moment or two. Warmth radiated down our bond when Lily recognized the gesture for what it was—a delay that allowed my queen to reply instead.

"Actually, I think that's a great idea! Thank you, Gretta," Lily offered kindly.

Only after Lily's reply did I respond as well. "Of course, Gretta. You know you're welcome anywhere in the castle."

Gretta dipped her head and winked at Lily, recognizing my deference as well. "Thank you. It is my continued honor to serve you both."

I took a step forward and reached for Gretta's hands. "We consider you family, if you haven't figured that out by now."

"Well, then... it's time I attend to our *family* meal. Dinner will be ready soon." She dipped her head and quickly left the room.

"Did I say something wrong?" Lily looked back at me with a creased brow. ""Why did she leave in such a hurry?"

"No, my love. She probably didn't want you to see her cry. She lost her family a long time ago, so any mention of..." My words trailed off.

I hadn't meant to bring up the war Lily's father had started. Nor was I sure if that's what truly drove Gretta to Dartmoor in the first place.

Lily

Thadius. *The bastard.* Every reminder of what he'd done still sickened me. And not just what he'd done to me, but to the entire fairy realm. Thank Goddess he was gone and that horrible time in our history was over.

Our history.

I truly did consider myself full Fae now, even if I did struggle with the fact that I was Queen.

Alder closed and locked the door, then pulled his shirt over his head and gestured toward the bathroom. "Join me?"

One look at him and I was reminded just how lucky I was. Standing over seven feet tall with broad shoulders, muscles to spare, and antlers gleaming in the candlelight amidst his dark hair, he melted my heart daily.

"Always," I replied, then removed my fur-lined coat, slipped out of my skirt and blouse, and undressed until I wore nothing but my boots.

"Wow, that's a look I could get used to." Alder now stood in the doorway with a towel wrapped around his waist.

"I could say the same." I sauntered past my husband with a smile on my face, coming to stand on the fur rug near the sink. "But don't get too excited. I just didn't want my feet to freeze. The onyx floors have been unforgiving since the weather turned cold."

A frown fell across Alder's face, his tone turning serious. "Lily, I'm so sorry. I didn't even think about that. Here, let me warm them up." He dropped to one knee and placed the palm of his right hand on the cold stone floor. Taking a deep breath, he closed his eyes, and I could feel the energy rise within him until a warm, familiar sensation rose to the surface.

He was using his elemental fire magic to heat the floors throughout the entire castle, and I stood there in awe.

"I didn't know you could do that!"

He looked up, meeting my shocked gaze. "Yes, there are a lot of ways to focus our element. But I don't want you to feel bad. You'll get the hang of it in time."

"Are you kidding me? You're not going to make me feel bad by doing what comes naturally to you just because I haven't mastered the element yet. In fact... I think *you* should be my new teacher!"

Alder rose from the floor and took my hands in his. "Really? You don't think you should continue practicing with your sisters? I thought you considered it necessary to work with all the elements at once. Besides, the last time we talked about it, you said I'd be more of a distraction than a help," he said with a devious grin.

I smiled wide. "Not if what we're doing isn't working. And you've had years with this element. It only makes sense." I slid out of my boots, kicking them into the corner of the bathroom, and reveled in the warm floor beneath my bare feet. "So, it's settled. Starting tomorrow, you'll be my teacher."

Alder wrapped his arms around my waist, pressing our bodies together as he walked us into the already steaming shower, thanks to his magic as well. "Are you sure you want to wait until tomorrow? There are a few things I'd like to teach you right now."

Suddenly, I was shivering again.

Four

Lily

Showered, sated, and unsurprisingly hungry, we returned to the dining room just as Gretta and the staff began to serve dinner. Braised lamb, roasted potatoes and carrots, and freshly steamed greens were presented with precision.

"This smells and looks delicious, as always." I nodded to the table in appreciation and received Gretta's usual wink.

We'd become great friends since my first night under her care, and I didn't even want to think about how things could've ended without her recent help with Fern. She had put us on the trail of the vilenflu flower, which inevitably saved us all. I was beyond grateful she decided to return to Dartmoor with us, though there wasn't much of a doubt. Gretta was family, and she'd follow Alder anywhere.

My heart tightened as she exited the room. I continually yearned to invite her to dine with us, but Alder had explained that would undermine her authority with the rest of the staff. While Gretta might appreciate the gesture, those who worked for her would not, and I would never do anything to make her job more difficult. So I picked up my fork and dug into the beautifully braised meat on my plate, savoring each bite.

"How do you think Aster will take it when you tell her you'll be studying with me instead?" Alder's voice filled the empty room, making the question feel heavier than it should.

"I'm not sure. Regardless, it's not up to her. She'll still be monitoring Iris and Fern's progress, and maybe without me there, Daisy will begin to gain some control, too."

"What do you mean? You think the two of you together is what's causing the issue?"

"No. Not necessarily. But if we are blocked because of Macha's influence, maybe us being apart will lessen that in some way." I took a sip of wine, swallowing past the lump in my throat.

Even I didn't believe it.

Alder took a few more bites, then met my eyes across the table. "Then I suggest we return to Ferindale tomorrow morning as usual. I'll turn the Guard's training back over to General Niasin, and you can let your sisters know what you've decided. Once everyone has been informed, we'll come home and get started in the garden, if that works for you?"

I nodded in reply, worried my voice would crack and give away the nervousness of my own plan. It was one thing to fail in front of my sisters, but quite another to fail in front of my husband and king. Maybe this wasn't such a good idea after all.

"Good, now let's enjoy our dinner and return to our room, so I can help work out all that stress you're carrying around."

I should have known. I couldn't keep anything from him, thanks to our bond. He would always know what I was feeling. Which was probably a good thing, since most of the time, *I* didn't even know where my emotions were coming from. One minute I felt confident and brave, and the next, I was a ball of anxiety. Alder was my anchoring force, and I was beyond grateful for his steadying presence in my life.

Feeling my love for him through our bond, he smiled and lifted his wine glass in the air. "To us."

"To us."

Lily

Stars sparkled against the night sky as we strolled through the garden for our after-dinner walk. Our meal was delicious as usual, but I wasn't ready to go to bed just yet. I needed to solidify my thoughts for the dreamwork I had planned, and nothing helped clear my head like a beautiful night under a glistening, open sky.

After a few minutes of silence as we meandered farther down the cobblestone paths, Alder asked, "Are you ready for bed, my dear?" His unending concern for my well-being echoed in his deep, soothing voice.

I nodded and let him lead me to our bedroom where he insisted I let him massage my neck. I was all too happy to oblige. His strong hands worked my shoulders, while his nimble fingers kneaded the exact spots to release my knots.

"Thank you. And I'm sorry you have to sleep here. But hopefully, it will only be for tonight." I stood from the couch and turned around, bending to kiss Alder on the cheek as he lay down on his side and curled his long legs beneath the blankets Gretta had provided.

"Please be careful, my love. I'll remain on the couch as you wish, but if something happens… I'm right here." He reached up and squeezed my hand, lending his strength to mine.

I crossed the room to the small round table next to the bed where Gretta had laid out all the ingredients I'd asked for. Now it was time to put them in place.

Pulling back the dark comforter and soft, deep green sheets, I tucked a large piece each of amethyst and moonstone beneath my pillow for anchoring and harmony, then climbed into bed. I stretched my arm toward the table again and grabbed the sachet of mugwort, chamomile, valerian root, and yarrow in my hand, bringing it to rest atop my heart. Closing my eyes, I took a few deeps breaths and began the process.

My intention was to initiate a lucid dream where I could recall and navigate the vision both Daisy and I had experienced. It wasn't something I *wanted* to do, but something I *needed* to do. I couldn't let my sisters down… or my kingdom. And I certainly couldn't let an old witch, or Goddess in this case, threaten our realm again.

On my next inhale, I re-formed the vision in my mind.

A crack split in a cobblestone path. Dark energy creeping out like insidious vines intent on choking the joy from our world. The sky darkened, and all the surrounding trees dropped their magically blackened leaves, blanketing the ground to look like a living, breathing pit of despair. The tree branches turned to spindly fingers and stretched threateningly in my direction.

I took another breath and focused solely on the crack.

It pulsed in a steady rhythm, spewing more darkness out every few seconds like belching lava. My chest tightened as I continued to stare—my heartbeat falling into sync with the sinister beat.

I yanked my attention from the ground and cast my eyes to the sky. Moonlight fought its way through the spell, piercing a sliver of silver light through the ominous clouds, allowing me to gain control of myself again.

I took a deep breath, breaking the pull.

Or so I thought.

Five

Alder

"Lily! Lily, wake up!" My panicked voice filled the room.

Lily strained to open her eyes and seemed to be struggling to readjust to the dim candlelight coming from the small table beside me. "What happened?" she asked into the dark.

"You started thrashing in your sleep." I picked up the candle holder, bringing its guttering flame to hover between us.

She followed my gaze to her hands and sucked in a sharp breath. They were tipped in black.

"Shit." She bolted upright. "This is bad."

We stared at her hands in unison, frozen for several disconcerting moments before she pushed out of bed and ran straight into the bathroom.

I followed her closely and watched as she flipped on the light, raced to the sink, and turned the knob. Steam rose as hot water flowed from the faucet, and she frantically scrubbed her hands, blinking through tears.

I quickly sat the candle holder on the counter and ran my hands down both her arms, coming to rest just above her wrists. "Scrubbing your skin raw isn't going to help. I think you need to consult my great-grandmother's book again." I reached past her and turned off the faucet. "Maybe there will be something in her fairy handbook to spells and salvation that can put an end to this."

She turned around, not bothering to wipe the tears from her eyes. "You're right. I'll look into it first thing in the morning," she said resolutely. "And... I'm sorry. I never expected it to go this way." She buried her head in my chest, and my heart broke.

I wrapped my arms around her and held her close. "It's okay, my love. I'm just glad I was here." My voice felt tight, still fraught with worry and fear, and I felt even worse when a pang of guilt radiated from her, slithering down our bond.

"In all my years as a witch, I've never experienced anything like this before. Any spells I ever cast came to me naturally and without any side effects—but that was then, and this is now... and everything has changed."

I remained quiet, not knowing what to say nor wanting to upset her further as she continued.

"As the full Fae Queen, my powers continue to grow and are proving to be more than I can handle. And as much as I practice and long for control, it only seemed to come in times of dire peril, which is utterly unacceptable and completely embarrassing."

Sniffling, she let me guide her back to our bed, and I climbed in beside her and pulled her against my chest. The tension in my muscles eased when her body curled into mine, and I could sense her thoughts starting to clear. Grateful to have her safely tucked within my arms, I kissed the back of her head, whispered I loved her, then forced myself to sleep. My support and belief in her were unending, but I knew when it came to owning her power, she'd need to figure this out herself.

Lily

The muted sunlight of Dartmoor filtered into the room from a small window beyond the couch. I blinked but remained still. Warmth radiated from behind me, and I felt the pressure of Alder's arm resting across my hip. We were safe and still in bed, thank the Goddess.

Relieved I'd managed a dreamless sleep, I took a deep breath and closed my eyes, not wanting to face the day just yet.

"Good morning." Alder's deep voice brought a smile to my face.

"Good morning. I'm sorry I woke you." I snuggled closer.

Pulling me tight, a sexy grumble reverberated from his chest. "Never apologize for that. Sleep is the one thing that separates us, and I'd gladly give it up if I could remain in your presence at all times." He nuzzled my hair, breathing me in and kissing my head.

Rolling to face him, I lifted my chin and brought my lips to his. "I feel the same way."

Snuggling beneath the blankets, we held each other tight, until I remembered—

Gasping, I pulled back and freed my hands from the sheets. They were still tipped in black. "Oh, Goddess. I'd hoped it was a nightmare."

Alder climbed out of bed, dressed quickly, and offered me my robe. "Take a shower. Get dressed. And I'll have Gretta prepare our breakfast. After that, we'll return to the library together and look through my great-grandmother's book." He kissed me again and walked to the door. "We'll get through this, Lily. Don't worry."

Don't worry? How could I not? A pulse of dark energy flared beneath my fingernails, festering like the vines spewing from the crack in my vision, as though it was testing the boundaries as it worked its way deeper and deeper into my blood with every passing moment.

"No. I want to address this now. Will you please return to Ferindale and bring Daisy here right away? I need to see if she experienced the same vision as me again last night."

Alder nodded. "Of course. I'll return as soon as I can."

Pulling a portal ball from his pocket, he tossed it on the floor then disappeared, already on his way to retrieve my sister.

I hoped she wasn't affected by my dreamwork, but somehow, I knew she was. I knew we were connected by Macha's energy, and I knew the Dark Goddess wasn't going to let us go.

I dressed in a rush, donning my usual leggings, over-sized sweater, and black leather boots, then made a bee-line for the library where we kept Gwenlyth Trelayne's ancient book of shadows. At this point, it felt like my only hope.

I approached the altar where it lay open, then froze, suddenly worried about touching it with my tainted hands. The prospect of infecting Alder's great-grandmother's spellbook with a single touch was too big of a risk. I'd have to wait for him to return.

Flopping into a nearby chair, I stared at my hands and was struck with a thought. *Perhaps my elemental magic could* burn *away the dark energy, turning Macha's hold to dust.* The moment the idea popped into my mind, heat flared beneath my skin—my magic rising to the call. But as usual, control was just beyond reach.

Sparks flew from my hands, spitting onto the floor and the surrounding rugs, lighting everything around me on fire. I jumped up and stomped at the flames, but some had already spread too far. I took a deep breath to call for help but choked on the rising smoke. Coughing into the crook of my arm, I moved toward the door but was blocked by a wall of flames.

This wasn't natural and not part of my magic.

I dropped to the floor and struggled to crawl toward the exit, barely making it a few feet as my eyes stung and my throat closed.

I could no longer see or breathe. Collapsing onto my side, I tried to call out again, but to no avail. Smoke and flames engulfed the room.

I didn't want to die. I wasn't ready to leave Alder, or any of my family for that matter. But most of all, I didn't want to fail Daisy and leave her at the mercy of Macha. Especially since all this started because *she* was trying to help save *me*.

Gasping to take a final breath, I welcomed the sting of tears and called out to Alder through our bond, desperate for him to hear me one last time. *I love you.*

Scorching heat and darkness pressed in around me, but a moment before everything went black, I saw a pair of small feet in delicate white shoes standing above me, and then… a piercing white light.

Fading fast, I closed my eyes and did the only thing I could: Prayed to my Goddess, and hoped for the best.

Six

Lily

The acrid smell of smoke filled my nose as I took a deep breath. Blinking into the white light, I pushed up from the ground—my hands hot against the smoldering floor.

"Alder?" I coughed out, struggling against the pain in my throat.

The white mist filled the room, and with no flames in sight, I wondered if this was heaven.

"Lily?" A female voice pierced the air, panicked and urgent.

"Daisy? I'm here!" I forced out.

Mist swirled in churning waves, flowing back in around two figures as they rushed to my side.

"Oh, my love… are you all right?" Alder's strong arms lifted me from the floor, holding me tight against his chest. "What happened here?" Pushing through the mist, he carried me into the hallway, and clean air rushed into my lungs. I could finally breathe again.

"I…" My voice was scratchy, the words struggling past raw cords and rough coughs. "I tried… to burn away… Macha's influence." I lifted my hands, and tears filled my eyes. Macha's mark remained, and my black-tipped fingers throbbed as if they had a heartbeat of their own.

"Lil, why would you do that? We're both still struggling to gain control of our elemental powers." Daisy's reprimand was spot on, and I now realized Macha's influence had reached my mind.

"I think she planted the thought in my head."

Goddess, this was bad.

Daisy was the one initially affected by Macha's dark energy, but now—because I thought I could face her on my own—I'd fully opened myself up to her as well. "I'm... sorry. I..."

"Enough. We can talk about this later." Alder's grip on me tightened. "Lily needs to rest. Gretta?" he called out, continuing when she entered the hall. "Bring up some water and medicinal tea for Lily's smoke-burned throat."

Gretta's eyes widened as she took in the scene, but with a clipped nod, she headed toward the kitchen, rushing to follow Alder's instructions.

"Let's get you back to bed, my love." He leaned down and kissed my head, easing my heart and mind despite the frantic, thunderous thoughts pounding between our bond. I knew he was frustrated with me, but more so, he was angry at the situation and terrified he'd almost lost me again.

Lily

By the time I woke, the sun had begun its descent. I swallowed slowly, fearful the pain in my throat remained, but was thankful when the motion was smooth and pain free.

"Are you feeling better?" Gretta's kind eyes met mine when I looked up to find a cup of steaming tea resting on the nightstand.

"Yes." I rubbed my throat. "Thank you."

Her ice-blue stare held mine, her shoulders sinking as she released a tight breath.

"What's wrong?" I asked.

Shifting in her chair, she dropped her head. Pieces of her long chestnut hair fell loose from her braid as she shared her concern. "With everything that Alder's gone through, I don't think he could survive losing you, too." She lifted her chin. "You have to be more careful, my lady."

I flinched at her words, but softened again as I watched a lone tear roll down her cheek. She was not only worried about Alder but had genuine concern for me as well. "Thank you, Gretta. I understand and will make sure to proceed with caution."

"I would like to be present if you're still planning to attempt to use Gwenlyth's book of shadows." She practically whispered the words, but the firm set to her jaw and the steeled look in her eyes left me little choice.

It was a given the book of shadows survived the fire, as it was magically protected in so many ways. And with my fingers still stained black, I'd be seeking its wisdom very soon.

"Of course. I would like that."

Gretta was an ancient Fae who had served the Dark Kingdom for centuries. Plus, she was the one who knew about that vilenflu flower that saved Fern and released all of our powers. If there was anyone I could trust to guide me through this... it was her.

With a thin hand, she gestured to the tea resting between us. "You should be fully healed after this final cup."

I scooted up in bed, resting my back against the elaborately designed headboard Alder had created when we moved back into the Dartmoor castle. He'd carved intricate reliefs of flowers and trees, with moons and stars scattered throughout. A portal tooled in perfect detail hovered in the corner, and there—silhouetted in the middle—was a Witch Queen and her Fairy King. It was the story of *us*.

I took the cup in my hand and sipped the hot liquid, noting a tinge of magic as it slid down my throat. "Thank you, Gretta. You certainly have a healing touch."

"Yes, well... I still think you need more rest. I can bring up some dinner, if you'd like."

"Is Alder here? If so, I'd love for him to join me." I was too tired to search our bond, and Gretta just smiled and dipped her head.

"I'll check to see if he's here. I'll be right back." She rose from her chair and exited the room, leaving me alone to think about all that had transpired.

I took another sip of tea, rubbing my throat as I swallowed. This could have been so much worse, and I was a complete fool for thinking I could handle this on my own. Once again, I felt like a young witch instead of the Fae Queen, and that had to stop. I may have been remorseful when my ideas and impulses didn't work out as planned, but that didn't mean I shouldn't own them and continue to do what I felt was right.

As soon as the door closed, I heard a familiar voice out in the hall. "Come in, Daisy," I called out.

My youngest sister raced into the room. "Oh, Gods, Lil. Are you okay?" She climbed into the bed and flung her arms around my neck.

"Yes, thanks to you and Alder for finding me when you did, and to Gretta's tea... I'll be fine."

She pulled back with tears in her eyes. "What were you thinking? I told you not to do it. It was a bad idea."

I took a deep breath and swallowed past the lump in my throat—it felt like everyone's disappointment had gathered and lodged there. "I was hoping to get a little more clarity on the vision we had, but when I woke and realized I'd made things worse, I wanted to take care of the mistake myself. That's it." I shrugged, hoping she'd understand I wasn't trying to contact Macha directly.

Even I wasn't that stupid.

Seven

Lily

After we'd finished a delightful dinner of freshly baked bread, perfectly-seasoned chicken, and heavenly potatoes au gratin, Gretta cleared our plates and made plans to meet Daisy and me back in the library to have another look at Gwenlyth Trelayne's fairy handbook to spells and salvation in an hour or so. Through magic, or the sheer will of Gretta and her staff, the library was clean and fully usable again.

I hadn't seen Alder since waking, but Gretta said he had checked on me often while I slept throughout the day and would be returning soon. Feeling better, I reached out through our shared bond but only felt a reassuring nudge—like a warm hug sent from very far away. He'd been spending a lot more time in Glenmiere, visiting Craven as often as he could, and I was sure he was there again now.

Our friendship with the Dark Elves had become invaluable over the last few months since we saved Fern and dispatched the crone. Craven had even offered to share more of their healing herbs they'd regrown after my father destroyed their crops during his tyrannical rule—another blight I was still struggling to get past.

No one blamed me for my father's behaviors or for any of the awful things he'd done, but I still carried the guilt within me. I never knew the insane egomaniac existed before last year.

Last year.

Only a handful of months was all it had taken for our lives to be completely turned upside down. And now this... dealing with the fallout from my sister's effort to save me and Macha's infectious influence.

My shoulders sank.

I really hoped we'd get a break soon.

As soon as the thought entered my mind, Daisy returned from the restroom. "Do you need help getting up?"

I shook my head, feeling again like the problem child. "No. I'm good. Just give me a moment." Pushing off the mattress, I rose from the bed, stifled a painful cough, and walked into the bathroom. Ignoring my black marred fingers, I turned on the sink faucet and gathered my hands beneath the water. Splashing my face, I kept my eyes closed and relished in the soothing relief the cool water provided against my hot sensitive skin. I prayed we would find some answers tonight.

"Thanks for being here with me." I smiled at my sister as we exited the room and headed for the stairs that would lead us back to the library.

"Of course." She slung her arm around my shoulders. "I'll always be here for you, Lil." Tears pooled behind my eyes, but Daisy's genuine smile kept them at bay. She really was the most selfless of us all. "I hate to ask, because I know we agreed not to tell Aster about the dream, but after what happened today, do you think we should let the rest of them know what's going on?" There was hesitation in her voice, but I knew the answer she was fishing for.

"Yes, but after we look through Gwenlyth's book of shadows, okay? I'll accompany you back to Ferindale, and we'll let the others know." I paused. "I also have to tell Aster that I'll be practicing with Alder instead, from now on."

Daisy stopped at the base of the stairs, her eyes going wide. "What?"

"Yes. It's something we decided last night. Alder is a master of his element, and I think his instruction would benefit me more than continuing to work aimlessly on my own or with our sisters."

Daisy's shoulders sank, and she cast her eyes to the floor.

"Don't be upset. It's just a theory and something we wanted to test this week. But now…" I held up my hands. "Who knows what will happen. And with all things considered, I think it's safer all around if I stay here with Alder… alone."

Daisy nodded but averted her eyes. Probably so I wouldn't see her cry.

"Come on. Let's meet Gretta and see what we can figure out." I hooked my arm in hers and pulled her into the library where Gretta was already waiting.

Gwenlyth's Trelayne's book of shadows sat closed on the altar in the corner of the room, waiting to be opened. Only a descendant in her line could use the book, or in my case, the next full Fae Queen of the entire realm, making Alder and I the only ones it would respond to.

I looked down at my hands again and was slammed with the same worry I had before. What if touching her book with my tainted fingers did something bad?

I looked to Gretta, who only nodded encouragingly, unaware of my concern.

Stepping up to the altar, I reached out with just one hand and eased open the cover with a feather-light touch. The book opened, thank the Goddess, but the pages were blank. Just like they'd been when we originally found it on Gideon's shelf.

The words had disappeared and were hidden again, and all my fears were confirmed. I could no longer use the fairy handbook to spells and salvation—at least not until I was free from Macha's influence.

This was a disaster.

Daisy picked up on my thoughts through our sisterly bond and replied, "Maybe you could have Alder look through it instead?"

"Maybe," I choked out.

Gretta led me to the couch and eased me down with a motherly touch. "Don't fret, my queen. We'll figure out a way to help you."

My queen.

What a joke! I was supposed to be this all-powerful fairy, and I couldn't do a single thing to help myself. I sank deeper into the couch and covered my face with my hands. "I can't do this anymore. I'm failing at everything… controlling my powers, being Queen, helping our kingdom. I have nothing to offer anyone, and I just want to go home."

Daisy and Gretta remained silent while I sobbed into my hands. I had let everyone down, and I truly didn't know what to do next. Then it hit me.

"We *must* go home. Back to Essex. Back to Hexx! I need to see if the shop and Mom can magically provide something that will help me figure this out!"

Daisy bounced on the balls of her feet. "That's a great idea, and literally what the shop is supposed to do… magically intuit its client's needs. Smart thinkin', Lil. When do we leave?"

I jumped up from the couch and walked to Gideon's desk, where I knew Alder kept a few portal balls in the top drawer. Retrieving one, I tossed it on the floor and smiled. "Right now! Gretta, please tell Alder where we went and that we'll be back as soon as I have some answers."

Gretta stared wide-eyed as Daisy and I disappeared through the portal, emerging in the next second at my favorite place in the world—the magical room in the basement of Hexx.

I was home.

Eight

Lily

With a hand on my heart and Daisy behind me, we climbed the circular stairs to the main floor of the shop. In the dim lantern light, it looked the same as always. A faded Persian rug lay in the center of the room, with Aster's books lining the shelves, and the scent of Fern's flowers and Daisy's herbs permeating the air. My candles and Iris's crystals glimmered along the far wall, for in its resting state, the shop represented a little of us all.

Tiptoeing across the hardwood floor, I resisted the urge to touch everything we passed. The purple front door stood as a silent sentry in the night, while the wooden desk we all shared in one form or another held a stack of orders and receipts. I wanted to linger and get to work. Anoint some candles with my sacred oils and prepare the boxes of orders that would ship out the following day. But with a nudge from Daisy, I was reminded of our task and headed for the third floor.

Cresting the top of the stairs, I called out to Mom, hoping she wasn't already in bed. "Mom?"

A shuffle from the living room caught my eye, and in the next second, Daisy and I were swept up into a familiar hug. "Girls! What are you doing here?" She didn't wait for us to answer. "Oh, my girls! You're home! It's so good to see you!" Kisses littered both our faces.

"Hi, Mom. It's good to see you too," I replied. As soon as she released us, we sank down onto the familiar deep emerald cushions of our couch and let out an exhaustive sigh. "I need your help... *We* need your help." I held up my hands and tried not to flinch when she gasped at my blackened fingers.

"Oh, no. Tell me everything." Mom pulled up a chair to sit in front of us and waited nervously for me to explain, but Daisy cut in before I could get a word out.

"It's my fault," Daisy said in a rush. "When Lily went missing, I used a spell in the crone's book to try to find her, and somehow called upon Macha—the Dark Fae Goddess the crone was loyal to. We thought I'd been purged of her influence, but when Lily used her powers to unlock our bond, she became infected too. Now, neither of us can control our elemental powers, and Lily has become even more... tainted. She can no longer use the previous Fae Queen's book of shadows, and we were hoping that maybe you and the shop's magic could point us in a direction that could help."

Mom remained silent, her eyes locked on my fingers.

"Oh, girls." She scooted forward, reaching for both our hands.

I hesitated, but she did not. She took our hands and squeezed them in hers, and I immediately felt relief.

It was short lived.

"I'm afraid there's nothing we can do from here." She stood and crossed the room. "As a matter of fact, I think now's a good time to tell you my plans."

Daisy and I swapped worried looks.

"I've been thinking about moving Hexx to Ferindale, and it seems the Goddess has revealed the reason why. I believe if we're in the realm where this happened, the shop's magic will have a better chance of guiding us to a solution."

I gawked at Daisy again, who sat wide-eyed and open-mouthed.

"I…" I stammered. "I didn't know moving the shop was even possible."

Mom walked to the kitchen and busied herself by putting on the kettle. "Well, yes. I believe now that the portals are open and the realms reconnected, it's just a matter of using the original spell to relocate and re-root the shop's magic. Since it originates from Ferindale, I don't see a problem."

Again, I looked to Daisy, who this time, just shrugged and smiled. I wanted to share in her enthusiasm, but I was drowning in concern. Of course, it would be great to have Hexx in the Fae realm, and more importantly…

"Does this mean you'll be living there with us, permanently?" I asked.

The tea pot whistled, heightening the moment.

"Absolutely! I've missed my girls." Mom didn't turn around, so I couldn't see her eyes, but a hitch in her voice had me thinking there was more to this decision than she was letting on. "Being with you all is the most important thing to me."

She returned to the living room with a tray of tea and set it on the side table, reclaiming her spot in the chair directly in front of us.

"I've spoken to Sybil and told her my plans, and she agreed to maintain watch over both our portals. With them linked now, she can send one of her Acrucian witches to check on ours regularly."

Silence fell across the house. Broken only by the sound of Mom pouring three cups of tea.

"Wait. So even though you're moving the shop, the building and the portal will remain intact?" Daisy asked.

"Yes, that's right. I simply planned to put up a sign that announces 'Permanently Closed' in the window. And once I ward the building, no one besides Sybil and her coven will be able to enter."

The word *simply* sounded too good to be true, but if anyone could do it, it was Mom. With Sybil's help, I had no doubt everything would be fine. Our families had been protecting this magic for centuries, and neither of them would fail in their duties now. But still...

"While this is all great news, I'm wondering, why now?" I asked.

Leaving our childhood home behind had been difficult for us all, but after learning of our Fae heritage and experiencing everything we had over the last year, I was thrilled Mom would be joining us there now. But another question remained... *Aster*. She was our only sister without any Fae blood running through her veins.

I looked around the room, noting a few of her books lying on the side table near the front window where she liked to read, then turned back to Mom. "What about Aster? Will she be staying in Ferindale as well?"

Mom's chin dipped as she took another sip of tea, her eyes dropping to the floor.

"What is it?" I asked.

I caught the slight shake to Mom's head before she answered, revealing her silent regret. "I haven't told her yet. I haven't told anyone besides Sybil and now the two of you, so I have no idea what Aster will choose to do." The china cup in her hand shook ever so slightly. "Losing Gideon was hard. *Very* hard. And as you know, as part of your protection, we were forced together in a way, and when the pact was made regarding your sisters and the specific timing of their births, I didn't think it would turn into what it did. But I loved Gideon, and I think he loved me, too." The cup clinked against the delicate saucer when she set it back down. "And while it will be hard to be there without him, it's no different than being here, alone, without all of you." She nodded to my fingers, their darkened tips sullying the beauty of her fine white china. "And this gives me a reason to speed things up."

Now I understood.

This had been building for a while and was part of Mom's way of dealing with her grief. My dilemma was the push she needed to see it through. "When do we get started?"

Aster

I crept down the hallway of the Ferindale castle, looking for a quiet place to read, or more preferably a quiet place to hide.

Fern and Iris remained in the sitting room, playing one of their dice games, and with Daisy joining Lily in Dartmoor, I finally had a moment to myself.

"Hello, beautiful." Craven's deep voice pulled a smile to my lips as I slipped into the shadows of the nearest alcove.

"I didn't expect you back so soon," I drawled, pressing my back against the cold marble behind me.

"Yes, well. I have some things to discuss with Alder and planned to meet him and your sister in Dartmoor tomorrow morning." He stepped forward, closing the distance between us. "But I will always make time to come see you."

The earthly scent of his fur cloak filled the small space, mixed with the crisp notes of pine and balsam, the cold, clean edge to the Dark Elf surrounded me, and as usual, I let myself fall victim to his charms.

Nine

Daisy

"Do you think we should call the others here first? Or at least inform Aster of your plans?" Lily asked the question I'd practically been choking on.

Mom returned to the kitchen—her refuge when things grew tense. "Unfortunately, no. There's simply not time. With your *infection* getting worse, and Macha's influence stifling Daisy's elemental powers, too, time is of the essence, I'm afraid."

Oh, my word! Springing something like this on Aster was not going to go over well. I was just glad it was Mom's idea and not mine. We already had enough tension lingering between us.

"So you just plan to show up in Ferindale and tell her then?" Lily asked with a raised brow.

"Well, yes. If she chooses to return here to Essex, she'll become the portal's keeper and live here alone." Mom shrugged, trying for nonchalance, but I could tell she was starting to stress. "Of course, I hope she stays with all of us, but it's entirely up to her."

"And what about the shop?" I asked, finally joining the conversation. "How will it react to being moved?"

Mom turned to me and took a deep breath, patience dotting her words. "Once I re-root the shop's magic in Ferindale, this place will go dormant. It will be just like any other building in Essex."

"Except for the fairy portal in the basement..." Lily piped up again, earning a huff from Mom.

"Girls, look. I know this must seem sudden and out of character, but I've been planning this for a very long time." Mom tilted her head, a sweet smile blooming across her face. "While I love our home and the life it provided us, I miss my girls more. And with Sybil and her coven protecting our portal here, our family will finally be reunited and can make a life together there, in Ferindale." Tossing a dishtowel over her shoulder, she walked to embrace us both. "This may seem like an ending, but in truth, it's only a continuation. Our duty here remains the same, but now we can protect both realms, united as a family in the united Fae Kingdom, thanks to Lily and Alder." She cupped both our faces. "That's something to be grateful for."

With a quick peck to each of our cheeks, she flicked her dish towel in the air. "Now, if you don't mind, let's get to work. There's lots to be done, and Sybil will be here in the morning to help me with the spell."

I turned around and scanned our humble home, taking in every nook and cranny. For years we'd known nothing beyond its walls, and we were happy. We were witches with a centuries-old duty and proud to be a part of that. But now… everything had changed. I swallowed past the lump in my throat and admitted, "I'm gonna miss this place."

Mom hugged me from behind, leaning her chin on my shoulder. "Me, too. But not as much as I've missed all of you."

Her familiar embrace settled my nerves, and I couldn't deny how great it would be to have her with us in the fairy realm. Especially if she thought moving Hexx there would help our current situation. Plus, since uniting the Light and Dark Kingdoms, Lily and Alder had welcomed the witch clans back into society, so having a specialty store that catered to their needs should go a long way in rebuilding that relationship. Of course, we'd have to monitor their purchases to make sure no one was attempting dark magic, but that should be easy enough. With the shop's magic, we should be able to keep track of any questionable purchases, too.

Bennett had assured us that by appointing a true elder council in each of the clans, there would be no chance of dark magic happening again. We were all skeptical, but he believed welcoming them back into the world they'd been separated from for so long was motivation enough. None of the witches would risk being banished again.

So, with Alder and Lily's approval, each clan had created their own council and swore an oath to the crown. They vowed to monitor their own witches to make sure another crone didn't come into power and ruin all of their lives. And they also swore to turn over anyone who attempted dark magic within their clan. It was a good deal for all involved, and with Bennett as the witches' liaison, I was confident it would succeed.

He'd become an integral part of the day to day workings at Ferindale, and I was proud to be his girlfriend.

"Mom, we'll need to make sure to track any questionable purchases in Ferindale. With the witches' return being so recent, it's part of their agreement not to practice dark magic. You'll have to keep records of that sort," I mentioned, wanting to help in any way I could.

"I'll be sure to work it into the re-rooting spell," she called out from her bedroom.

Lily looked up from the stack of books in her hand. "I can't believe you have the original casting spell for the shop and never told us."

Mom poked her head out of the door and smiled. "We all have our secrets, dear."

With a quick wink, she returned to cleaning her room, leaving Lily and I to sort through the rest. We spent the next five hours rooting through books, clothes, trinkets, and keepsakes, making sure we packed anything we thought any of our sisters might want or need. We considered using a spell, but decided this had to be done by hand. It was intimate. Special. And memories lingered in every item we touched. Now they would get a new life, just like all of us.

Mom stood in the doorway with three overstuffed bags slung over her shoulders and arms. "Almost done."

She glanced down at Lily's fingers with a look of concern that neither of us missed. This move wasn't on a whim, but it was obvious she thought we needed to get back to the fairy realm as fast as we could.

Lily

Sybil arrived at three in the morning, rousing Daisy and me from the couch.

Untwisting our legs, we both yawned as we sat up. Sleep still lay heavy in our bones, but it was time.

"Hi, girls. It's good to see you both."

Daisy and I stood and gave Sybil a hug.

"It's good to see you, too." I smiled, taking in her long red hair and shining lavender eyes.

She hadn't changed a bit.

Mom came out of her room carrying a small leather book bound with a thin leather cord. I wasn't sure why I expected the magic spell that protected an entire network of fairy portals to be contained in a large, oversized book, but I did.

Mom said nothing as she unwound the cord and nodded for us to follow her downstairs.

Descending the steps of my childhood home felt different this time. Like the house itself knew we were leaving and was mourning, too.

My footsteps grew heavy as we reached the wooden door at the bottom of the spiral stairs in the hidden basement of our magical shop.

With a twist of the metal key, Mom unlocked the door.

The blue portal still stood behind the scrolling metal gate, pulsing just as brightly as I remembered. Setting my bags on the floor, I walked to my favorite rock near the small pool along the wall's edge, sat down, and dipped my toes into the water. The motion felt familiar, but the emotions they evoked were completely new.

A wave of sadness overwhelmed me, doubling me over.

"Lily, what's wrong?" Daisy rushed to my side.

"I'm not entirely sure." I clutched my chest.

The water at my feet began to ripple, like something was trying to emerge from its depths.

Mom walked to my side, bent down, and laid her hand on the surface. The water calmed immediately, and thankfully, so did the ache in my chest. She looked up at me with a sad smile. "Being Queen means you're connected to the fairy realm like never before. You feel the magic in your veins, but it's also reflected in your emotions. The portal room can sense that and is mimicking your distress."

I frowned. For years, this was the place I found solitude. Peace. And now, because of my *title*, my emotions were having a negative effect on it? I dropped my head. "Sometimes, I wish I wasn't Queen."

Daisy bent down, meeting my eyes. "Lil, don't say that. You've done so many wonderful things, and your people love you. The entire Fae realm wouldn't be the same without you."

I looked down at my tainted fingers and shook my head. "I don't know, Dais. Maybe they'd be better off."

Ten

Lily

"Oh, for goodness' sake." Sybil took me by the hand—unfazed by my tainted fingers—and pulled me off the boulder and out of my stupor. "I know this feels like an ending, but you're wrong. You becoming Queen has been the best thing that could have ever happened to you *and* the realm. Yes, it's hard, and there will continue to be many lessons to learn. But you, and you alone, are the only one who can maintain peace and bring balance to a world that's been divided for centuries." She met my eyes, and her words of wisdom took root. "Alder needs you, and you need him. Plus, isn't this what you want? For your mother to be there with you all?"

I nodded, grateful for the wakeup call.

"Good. Then let's get started. I promise, my coven will take good care of the shop and portal from this side. You have nothing to worry about."

I looked to Mom, who gave me a reassuring nod as well. I knew coming here would be hard, but it was time to say goodbye to my old life and embrace my *real* life, with Alder, anew.

"What do you need us to do?" I asked.

Mom pointed to the floor, marking a straight line with her finger. "Line up here in front of the portal."

Daisy and I stood together with Mom next to me and Sybil next to her.

Mom began reading from the small book, then she and Sybil whispered together, weaving the spell.

My ears started to ring.

Like an invisible bubble collapsing from the top of the building, the fairy magic fell around us until all that was left was an impenetrable field around the portal room itself.

I closed my eyes and knew once we stepped through the portal, we'd emerge into the new Hexx in Ferindale. I could feel it in my bones.

Taking one last look around the secret room, I took a deep breath, committing my life here to memory, then picked up my bags and led the way home.

The building I arrived in looked exactly like the Hexx store we just left, and I couldn't be happier. Shelves lined with each of our wares: my candles, Daisy's herbs, Fern's flowers, Iris's crystals, and of course, Aster's books each sat mingled together for now. The shop's magic wouldn't work until we were all here together and truly "open for business".

"Wait... who will take over my candle shop?" I asked. "Obviously, I cannot be here to run it anymore."

Mom set her bags down on the round mandala rug and slung an arm around my shoulders. "I changed the spell so the store will permanently house all our wares together and allow any number of customers inside at once."

My eyes widened as I looked around again. Seeing and feeling the rightness of the update in the early morning light of Ferindale brought a smile to my face. "Good. I think that will serve the community well."

Mom winked at me and continued sharing her plans. "Aster and I will manage the store for the most part, allowing you and your sisters to continue your training."

Training.

I took a deep breath, remembering I still had to tell Aster I'd chosen to start working with Alder instead. Hopefully, Mom's arrival and her renewed duties at Hexx would be enough of a distraction that I wouldn't have to hear about why she thought it was a bad idea. Besides... I didn't think it was.

Mom squeezed my shoulders again, refocusing my thoughts. "Can you use your bond and ask the rest of your sisters to join us here?"

Daisy bounced on the balls of her feet in front of us. "I already did!"

I wandered the store, touching each shelf and trinket with a sense of revere. Minutes later, Aster, Fern, and Iris came tumbling through the front door and into Mom's arms.

"I can't believe you did it," Aster confessed—surprised but seemingly happy. "You and Hexx are really here!"

"Yes, well... it was time." Mom took a moment to look at each of her girls, but her eyes lingered on me.

I tucked my hands behind me and walked to where our green high-back chair now sat against the wall and took a seat.

The bell above the door rang, and all our heads snapped toward the front of the shop.

"Well, well... what a wonderful sight to see." Alder's deep voice filled the room and melted my heart. "Welcome, Camellia. It's good to have you here."

Mom smiled and dipped her head. "Thank you, Your Majesty. It's good to be back with all my girls. Let me show you around." Winding her arm through Alder's, she led him deeper into the store, pointing out all the items we stocked and sold while explaining her new plan of operation.

Daisy meandered over to me, standing with her back against the wall. "So when are you going to tell Aster what you've decided?" she whispered.

I glanced at my older sister across the room, now standing and talking to Alder and Mom. "Probably later today or tomorrow morning, before our regular training session begins." I swallowed hard.

"How do you think she'll take it?" Daisy's voice caught on a laugh.

"About as well as you'd expect."

"What's with all the whispering over here?" Fern came around the end of the counter, her hand sliding across the new marble as she joined us.

"Nothing. Just wondering how I'm going to break some news to Aster. That's all."

"What news?" Iris added from behind Fern as she walked up with a small cluster of amethyst in her hand.

"Geez… can a girl get some space?" I pushed out of the chair, shoved my hands in my pockets, and walked over to where Alder, Aster, and Mom now stood. "I think I've had enough excitement for one day. Are you ready to go home? I could still use some more sleep." I nudged Alder with my hip.

"Of course." He smiled, taking the hint and pulling a portal ball from his pocket.

We said our goodbyes and exited the shop, but not before Mom caught my eye one last time. With a final hug, she whispered in my ear, "I want to see you back here later this afternoon."

I dipped my chin, acknowledging her request but already dreading what was to come. My plans to speak with Aster or begin my training with Alder was going to have to wait. Mom was making it clear: this was something we needed to deal with now.

Eleven

Alder

Lily followed me through the portal I produced, and we emerged back in Dartmoor castle.

"That was a hasty exit. Everything okay?" I wrapped my arm around her waist and guided her to the dining room table where scents of freshly baked bread, sweet jams and jellies, and an array of succulent fruit wafted through the air. Her stomach rumbled in response. "I figured you could use some breakfast before lying down to rest."

She gazed up into my eyes, a look of love blooming on her face. "Thank you. This is perfect. I'm glad you know me so well." She slid into the high-back, wooden chair at the head of the table and took a sip of the freshly-squeezed juice. "And to answer your question…" she sighed. "I didn't feel like getting into it with Aster or the rest of my sisters about, well… *everything*."

"You mean the darkness and switching up your training?"

She nodded.

I sank my fork through a stack of fluffy pancakes. "I don't see why either is a big deal. You're the Queen. You can do whatever you want, and it cannot be questioned." I slid the layered bite between my lips, pulling the fork back out with a pop to punctuate my point.

Lily's self-doubt and continued struggles regarding her powers and becoming Queen plagued her daily. So whenever I could, I made the conscious effort to let her know how much I believed in her and would continue to do so until she believed in herself, too.

She choked on a laugh. "That might work with the subjects of our realm, but we're talking about my sisters, here. The same rules do not apply."

"Well, maybe they should." My fork clanged against the plate, and I took a sip of water from my wooden cup, swallowing hard. "They're all our subjects now. Especially since officially declaring they'll be staying in Ferindale permanently."

Lily raised an eyebrow. "I don't think Aster has *officially declared* anything."

"Actually..."

My sentence trailed off as Gretta entered the room. "Sir, Craven has arrived."

Right on time.

I smiled and waved for Gretta to show him in.

"I thought you just left Glenmiere? What is he doing here?" Lily asked.

"Lily!" Craven's boisterous voice boomed into the dining hall. "It's so good to see you again."

The last time she saw Craven, aka the brute as she liked to call him, was only a few weeks ago when he came to Ferindale to attend one of my training sessions with the Guard. Craven had been instrumental in exposing the crone, and of course, stayed as a welcome guest afterward to attend our wedding.

"It's good to see you, too! What brings you to Dartmoor?" Lily asked.

My wife's eyes narrowed on me as *the brute* glanced in my direction, and I gave a slight shake of my head.

"All right, you two. What's going on?" Lily demanded, not missing a thing.

Craven took a seat beside me at the table. "I take it you haven't told her yet."

I lifted my chin confidently, but my eyes remained warily locked on my queen's. "No. I have not."

"Then let me be the first to announce the good news." Craven pushed dramatically from the chair and stood with his arms out wide. "I've entered into courting negotiations with the King, so that I may ask Aster to be my wife."

Lily's jaw hit the floor.

I'd let her believe my visits to Glenmiere had been about strengthening our ties with the Dark Elves, but it was clear now that wasn't the only reason. Craven was old-fashioned, and from the looks he'd been giving Aster every time he visited Ferindale, I was surprised Lily hadn't realized something was going on between the two of them before now.

I can't believe you didn't tell me, she sent into my mind.

All I could muster was a mental shrug, hoping Craven would explain himself and save me from the couch again.

Craven had initiated *courting negotiations* with me—the customary fairy tradition when choosing your bride—a few months ago. And though during my multiple visits to Glenmiere where I explained that's not how things were done nowadays, he remained adamant.

Does Aster know? Are they already a thing? Lily's words pelted my mind with a bite.

It's not for me to say. I hoped she could hear the underlying apology in my words.

Fuming, she met my gaze, but held her tongue, turning to Craven instead. "I suppose congratulations are in order, then." She stood and walked around the end of the table, giving Craven a hug. "And I assume you and Aster are already involved?" Craven's cheeks reddened. An odd sight to see on the hulking Elf. "I'll take that as a yes," Lily said kindly, admitting to me privately, *I can't believe she hid this from me!*

Yes, well, since first meeting your sister, I've known her to be a private person, and this is her *story to tell.*

Lily took a deep breath, and I tried to hide my smile. *Damn your maturity,* she sent. *You're right. Your royal duty to our people should always shine through, even if it does trump my family issues.*

Taking a step back and focusing on Craven again, Lily stretched her arms out wide. "Well, then I supposed there's only one thing left to say..." She tilted her head up to meet his eyes. "Welcome to the family."

Craven chuckled and returned to his seat. "Yes, well, let's not get ahead of ourselves. I haven't even asked her yet." He met my eyes across the table. "I still have to get approval from our king."

Lily's eyes went wide. *You haven't given him permission yet?*

The corner of my lips ticked up. *Believe it or not, I was going to talk to you about it first.*

She rolled her lips between her teeth and dipped her chin. *Go ahead. Craven's a great guy, and if he can put up with Aster, more power to him.*

I looked to Craven. "Your Queen gives her approval, and therefore, so do I." I lifted my wooden cup in the air, making the announcement seem more official, but all I could do was laugh.

"I can't believe you and Aster are a thing. I'm so happy for you both!" Lily reiterated.

Craven grinned, but then lowered his head, his eyes dropping to the table. The mood shifted in the room, and after a few moments he spoke again. "Yes. Well, it's been a very long time since I felt this way about someone."

Lily looked to me, and I suddenly found my plate to be the most interesting thing in the room. Obviously, this fell into the *his story to tell* category as well, but I knew in that moment we both wondered what Craven's story might be.

Twelve

Lily

In the dim light of early afternoon, I rose from my nap and dressed for the day again. Gretta had already brought a late lunch to my room as requested, and within minutes I was ready to return to Hexx and begin the work with Mom to remove Macha's influence once and for all.

At least that was the hope.

I had no idea what she had in mind, but I would try anything, and I was almost certain that's what Alder feared the most.

"Please be careful," he said for what felt like the fiftieth time.

"I will." I cupped his cheek and rose onto my toes to give him a kiss.

He placed his hand over mine and met my eyes with a piercing gaze, stalling my affection. "Lily, I'm not kidding. *Please* be careful. I cannot lose you, and even though I hate to admit it, more importantly, the realm cannot lose its queen."

"I'll be fine." I turned away and reached for the portal ball lying in the glass dish on my dresser. "Honestly, there's no place safer for me to do this. And no one better to help than my mom." I swallowed the words, hoping he believed them, but honestly, I wasn't sure if I did myself.

Mom was a powerful witch, and with her duty and involvement with Gideon, she clearly had more knowledge about the fairy realm than any of us girls ever realized, but still… I wish I knew what she had planned and how she thought it might help.

"I'll be back before you know it, and we'll start my training this afternoon. Sound good?" I tossed the portal ball on the floor before he could argue, but Alder grabbed my hand, stopping me from stepping through.

"I love you, Lily. No matter what happens, please remember how much I love you."

I swallowed hard. "I love you, too."

I turned away, stepped through the waiting portal, and emerged back inside Hexx—its familiar scents of lavender, mint, and bergamot welcoming me like no other place in the world could.

"Mom?" I called out.

"In here." Her voice echoed from the back room, causing another wave of emotions to roll over me.

My mom was here, in Ferindale, and would remain so until her dying days.

The thought stopped me short.

With my half-sisters' latent fairy powers unlocked, the four of us would have extended lives, like the rest of the Fae… but not Mom and Aster. They were fully human, and for the first time, I wondered what living here might mean for them.

I pulled another portal ball from my skirt pocket, tossed it behind me, and yelled, "Be right back!"

I reemerged in our bedroom and practically crashed into Alder's chest.

"Lily, what's wrong?" My husband rushed toward the portal, scrambling me behind him and expecting a threat to follow.

"Nothing. I'm fine." I stepped out of his protective shadow, flopped down onto our bed, and covered my eyes with the crook of my arm. "I just thought of something I needed to ask you about right away."

The wooden legs of the desk chair screeched across the onyx floor as Alder pulled it up to the edge of the bed. "What is it?"

The wobble in my chin had him scooting even closer.

I sat up. "I want to know what will happen to Mom and Aster since they're the only true humans living in the fairy realm." I didn't think the changelings would count, assuming they would have died out when the crone did.

A tiny gasp was the only indication I'd caught him off guard, but it was enough to set my worries alight. "I knew it. They're not truly going to be able to stay here, are they?"

Alder grabbed both my hands and ran his thumbs along each of my wrists—a calming effort to keep me from spiraling. "Lily, calm down. Of course your Mom and Aster can stay in the fairy realm. Being fully human only means they'll live out their lives just as they would on Earth. Aging and dying as a normal human would."

I took a deep breath. *At least that's something.*

The kindness in my husband's eyes portrayed he knew exactly what I was feeling. He squeezed my dark hands. *Once we get past this issue, we'll look through my great-grandmother's book to see if there's anything mentioned about humans living in the fairy realm.*

I nodded, thankful for our bond, and more so that I found a man who understood me so well. He knew I wouldn't let this go.

Alder stood from the chair and pulled me into his arms. "All right, now let's get you back to Hexx, so we can get this matter taken care of." He squeezed my hands again, confirming he was in just as big of a rush to rid me of Macha's influence as I was.

"Agreed." I reached up and kissed him on the cheek, this time finishing the motion before stepping toward the new portal he'd produced. I looked back over my shoulder. "No matter what happens, please remember, I love you so much."

His eyes widened as I stepped into the shimmering white light. I was determined to get this done and return to him whole, ready to face the next challenge of being Queen.

"Where did you go?" Mom stood behind the long counter that made up Hexx's main workspace, tossing herbs into a stone mortar.

"I needed to pop home for a moment. All is well." I smiled and meandered closer, wondering what ingredients she chose to begin with, but the closer I came, the faster my smile faded.

Mom caught the look on my face and shook her head before I could say anything. "Don't worry, the henbane will only stun you. But we need your mind *and* your magic subdued for this to work."

I gasped and stumbled back. "You're going to subdue my magic... again?" A hollow ache formed in my chest. I'd forgiven Mom for suppressing my fairy magic all those years ago—understanding why it needed to be done, but a sharp sting of betrayal flared deep within me as I thought about my childhood and how I was forced to live a lie.

Fear coursed through my veins, freezing me in place, until the warmth of Mom's hand on my arm thawed my frigid thoughts.

"Lily, I would never hurt you or threaten your role as queen. This is just a precaution and the only way I know how to break through Macha's influence." She wrapped her arms around me, pulling me in for a hug and reminding me of all the love she'd bestowed on me over those same years.

I stifled a sob and nodded against her shoulder then, blinking through watery eyes, I looked back at the counter and the ingredients she'd prepared. "Tell me what I need to do."

Thirteen

Lily

Mom went through the same motions I'd seen her follow hundreds of times—grinding the herbs, steeping the kettle, preparing the cup with a pinch of lavender to aid the success of the spell—but when she handed me the elixir to drink, I froze.

"It's all right, honey. I'm right here." She guided me to the couch in one of the back alcoves, gesturing for me to take a seat. "You'll need to finish the cup entirely, then simply lie down. You should feel your body relaxing, and—" Her pause caused my heart to race. "You may feel, *heavy*. Like there's something weighing you down, but don't worry… that's to be expected."

To be expected. I took a deep breath and reached for the cup.

The bitter notes of henbane made me cough, but once my pallet adjusted to the herb, I finished the tea like any other. Drinking to the dregs, I handed the cup back to Mom and lay down as instructed.

The henbane's first effect was purely physical. My limbs felt heavy as Mom had indicated, and a dull pain began to hammer in my head. Needle pricks dotted my arms and legs, like a thousand bee stings happening all at once. The spell to remove my magic was not going to be fun.

I strained to open my eyes, forcing myself to focus past what I could only imagine were my very enlarged pupils. I could barely see. The outlines of objects were hazy at best, obscured in a thin mist, with the bulk of their makeup nothing more than a tiny black dot.

My heart raced, and the shop I loved became a house of nightmares. Small animals peered out from behind the books on the shelves, looking at me keenly with contorted grimaces and staring at me with terrified eyes. A cloud of mist crept across the floor, intent on devouring me, I was sure. I pulled my legs up tightly to my chest and crouched into the corner of the couch as far as I could go.

"Lily, it's okay. It's just the hallucinogenic effects of the tea. I'm right here."

While I heard Mom's words and felt the warmth of her hand, my mind could only process the mass of black smoke that now threatened to envelope the floor. Like the gaping maul of a witch's cauldron, it was going to swallow me whole.

I slammed my eyes closed and gripped my head in both hands. *It's not real. It's not real.*

A drip hit the top of my head and when I looked up, water was flowing, dark and blood-red. The room had opened up, and the sky was filled with a mass of fluid, formless creatures emerging from the dark depths beyond. A buzzing rang in my ears, nonsensical and wrong, yet the scrambled words possessed some hidden meaning meant only for me.

"Lily, you must focus. Break through the delusion and come back to me." Mom's voice was my only tether.

I fought the urge to close my eyes again, picking instead one point in the distance to concentrate on—a large deer standing regally atop a crest between two wise oaks.

Alder.

His name floated through my mind, and the longer I stared, the clearer my vision became. The mass of creatures retreated, and the smoke on the floor faded away, until all that was left was my husband in his awe-inspiring animal form, had he been a full shifter.

"That's it. You're doing great."

A deep ache formed in my chest, tight and fast, like a fist squeezing my heart from the inside out. Mom's whispers grew louder, and the pain grew with them. I screamed, flinging myself across the couch as if I could escape the excruciating work of the spell.

A flash flared behind my eyes, and a memory assaulted me. A memory of when I was young and in an immense amount of pain— the same pain I was feeling now.

A vision of our original living room clouded my mind, and standing over me were Mom, Sybil, and Aster, whispering a chant with tear-filled eyes. I could hear my own youthful screams from far, far away.

How could they do this to a child?

Back in my adult body, I writhed again as the effects of the spell fully took hold.

"There, there. You're okay. It's all over." Mom's gentle touch grounded me, yet I couldn't help flinching away.

"How could you do this to me?" The question slipped past my lips before I could stop it.

Mom stumbled back as if my words had landed a physical blow. "Lily, I'm so sorry. I thought you agreed this was the only way."

I sat up, cradling my head in my hands and struggling to catch my breath. "I'm sorry. Yes. I do agree. It's just that I saw…" How could I be mad at something that happened so long ago, and for good reason, too? I knew the story—how Gideon had fled Ferindale with me to save me from my biological father and the crone. And how they had to suppress my fairy magic so we would remain safe and undetected—but that didn't make it any easier to witness now. "I saw a memory of when you performed this spell on me as a child, and…"

Tears pooled in my mother's eyes. "Oh, Lily. I'm so sorry. I never imagined the spell would connect you to the past." Mom knelt in front of me, lifted my chin with the crook of her finger, and met my eyes with a sympathetic gaze. "That was one of the hardest days of my life, but unfortunately, I'd do it all over again since it worked and kept you protected for so very long."

Safe, yes. But completely disconnected to who I truly was. "I understand what had to be done, but at times, this life…" I gestured to the fairy realm as a whole. "It's still so new. It seems like a dream. I only wish I had learned the truth sooner."

Mom stood and offered me her hand. "You know what they say, hindsight is 20/20." Her eyes fell, and a look of sadness settled over her features. "There are so many things I'd do differently, if given the chance."

I rose from the couch, gripping Mom's hand as I wavered on my feet. "Whoa."

"Yes, sorry. It will take a minute to adjust to being without your magic."

My heart clenched, and I instinctively reached for the well inside me and felt nothing. I collapsed back onto the couch, realizing this was going to be so much harder than expected.

Mom sat down next to me and rested her hand upon my knee. It was like she needed to make sure I was still there, or more likely, realized she was the only thing keeping me grounded in this moment.

I closed my eyes and pictured the well in which my magic usually resided. There was an emptiness to it, but the longer I stared, the more I could see. Waves rippled in the pool, like they had back in Hexx before we left home, and suddenly, the well grew to the size of an ocean, and I was flooded with a surge of powerful magic.

"Ahhhh!!!" I tossed back my arms and head as a white light poured from deep within me, filling the entire room. The last thing I heard was Mom's awestruck gasp before darkness claimed me again.

Fourteen

Lily

"There, there. You're all right."

I recognized Mom's voice, clear and centered, but could sense others in the room as well.

"What happened?" I sat up with my head in my hands, blinking until the shop came into focus—along with the rest of my sisters, whose faces all seemed to be etched with varying levels of concern.

"The spell didn't work." Mom scooted closer, taking my hand. "Or maybe it did." She lifted our joined fingers into the air, and all were clean and smooth.

No longer did Macha's magic stain my fingers, or from what I could tell, my soul.

"It did work!" I stood and spun in a circle. "I can feel it. I'm free. But how?"

"I'm not entirely sure. I thought my spell worked, but your magic seemed to burn right through it… and through Macha's influence as well." Mom smiled brightly, but her eyes still carried a hint of wariness.

"I tried to burn out Macha's influence before, but instead, I set the house on fire. I wonder why it worked this time?"

The bell above the door rang, and in walked my husband and Gretta. "Because your magic was threatened, and your *essence* wouldn't allow that to happen." *I'm so glad you're okay, my love*, he added privately through our bond.

Thank you. Me, too.

"My *essence*?" I asked out loud.

"Yes. As the Fae Queen of the entire realm, you've inherited more than just the title. You now hold our world's very essence inside of you, according to my great-grandmother's book."

Gretta stepped forward, holding Gwenlyth Trelayne's book of shadows in her hands. She opened it, and I gasped. The words had returned, and I could read it again.

"I did as Miss Daisy suggested and had Alder look for a cure in the book when he returned, and while there was nothing specific about your *affliction*, we did find this…"

In the center of the open page was an elaborate tree, full and blooming with life on top, while below the surface lay a beautifully entangled twist of roots cocooning a woman's body. The inscription read, "*From essence to embers, and embers to dust. A Queen will always do as she must.*"

"It goes on to say that as the rightful queen of a united realm, you're now connected to this world. Its essence dwells within you, and unless—like my great-grandmother chose to do—you voluntarily give that power away, you will forever be protected because of it."

I stood awestruck, gawking between the book and my husband's face. Pride shone in his eyes, and with it, a flurry of questions crashed into my mind. "I need to sit down." I gestured for everyone to join me and waited until chairs and ottomans were slid into place and all had claimed a seat. "While I'm grateful, to be sure, I don't exactly understand. If my *essence* protects me when my magic is threatened, then why was Macha able to infect me in the first place?"

Alder slid forward in his seat. "In each of those instances, *you* had reached out, voluntarily, when using your magic. Once you opened yourself up by doing so, Macha's influence was able to take hold." He nodded, like that explained it all.

"Wait. So you're saying, if I do nothing—cast no spells, no longer call on my magic in any circumstance—I will always have a natural defense because I carry this world's essence inside me?"

Alder tilted his head from side to side. "Yes and no. You can still do magic and cast spells, but only when the root of your magic is threatened will your Fae essence kick in."

Mom sobbed from the corner. "I'm so sorry. I had no idea my spell was threatening her in that way."

I rose from the couch, crossing the room in a flash. "Mom, don't do that. You have nothing to be sorry for. Your spell is what triggered my essence and saved me. It was the right thing to do."

All my sisters nodded in agreement, their eyes welling with tears. There were no more secrets between us. They all knew about Macha now.

"Yes, well. Whether it was my spell, your essence, or the shops magic giving it a boost, I'm just glad you're okay." Mom kissed my forehead and wiped away her tears.

I looked across the room and caught Daisy's eye. Her slight shrug and the tiny quirk to her lips spoke volumes. She wouldn't be afforded the same result, and she knew it. She wasn't full Fae, or the Queen, but we still had to try.

"Since we're all here, can we try to release Macha's spell on Daisy as well?" I nodded in my little sister's direction. "Are you ready?"

With a nod of her head, she lifted her chin, brave as always.

Lily

Settled in a circle, we each held a smudge stick in hand—the ceremonial burning of dried sage was an honored tradition of witches, fairies, and humans alike. Fully centered in my power, I pulled on my fire element and lit the bundles with ease. Everyone smiled at the small accomplishment, but it was Alder's voice in my head that warmed my heart.

I'm so proud of you. Without the taint on your magic, it comes easily, yes?

Yes, and I'm so grateful.

Mom handed Daisy the elixir, giving her the same instructions I'd received. "You'll need to finish the cup entirely, then simply lie back. You should feel your body relaxing, and you may feel heavy, like there's something weighing you down, but don't worry... that's to be expected."

"And get ready for some crazy hallucinations," I added. "It helps if you pick something to focus on to guide you through."

What did you focus on? Alder's thought carried a teasing sensuality with it, but he had no idea how much the thought of him had helped me.

You, of course. But in a fully-shifted state. I took a deep breath, remembering the power and majesty he possessed. *You were beautiful and will always be my anchor.*

Love radiated between us, tinged with a hint of sadness. In reality, he would never be able to fully shift since his father was Fae, making him only a half-shifter.

Daisy coughed and sputtered after drinking the tea, pulling me back to the present. But unlike my experience, she didn't seem to be in pain or scared in any way, and I couldn't help but wonder why.

"Is it working?" I asked tentatively.

Fern's eyes widened. "Yes. Can't you feel it? The connection to her magic is shrinking."

I focused on our sisterly bond and noticed the same thing. Daisy's inherent magic was almost gone, along with her air element. She was being laid bare, metaphysically speaking, and I hoped Mom was ready for what was to come.

Fifteen

Lily

Daisy didn't move. Didn't make a peep. Until Mom approached with a lit smudge stick in hand. Only then did a small moan escape her lips as she began to writhe beneath the cleansing smoke.

Mom continued to bathe her in the healing mist while whispering a spell none of us could hear. Whatever she was doing seemed to be working, so we all remained quiet, watching with bated breath.

Tiny beads of black-tinged sweat formed on Daisy's skin—Macha's residual influence being pulled to the surface, no doubt. Thankfully, there wasn't much, which meant my previous efforts *had* mostly worked.

The five of us stood still while Mom continued to weave her spell.

Daisy screamed at the same time the bell above the door rang.

I turned and gasped as Bennett entered the shop and made his way between us. "What is this?" he demanded.

Daisy's body thrashed against the pillows, as if reacting to Bennett's presence. A thick, black mist erupted from her mouth while Mom did her best to subdue her body.

Cords of Macha's magic poured from Daisy's skin, stretching out in thick tendrils and reaching directly for Bennett.

"I think it's reacting to your shadow magic. You have to leave! Now!" I could only hope my assumption was right.

Bennett stood still, gawking between myself and Daisy, clearly frozen in fear.

"Go!" I pointed my finger back at the door. "I'll come get you when it's over."

Bennett's eyes darted wildly between the woman he loved, with the strange dark magic pouring out of her, and the shop's purple front door.

"Go!" I shouted again.

He turned hesitantly and stomped from the shop, his footfalls as heavy as my heart.

As soon as the bell rang, Macha's energy settled, proving my point. Daisy's body slumped against the pillows on the floor, passed out but still alive.

"What the hell was that?" Fern asked, iterating what we were all thinking.

"I don't know." Mom blew on her sage bundle, reigniting the embers until they were blazing red again.

The rest of us joined in, swiping the smoke from our bundles up and down Daisy's body as more and more dark energy beaded on her skin.

I'll go after Bennett and explain, Alder sent into my mind.

I nodded without looking up.

Macha's energy *had* been drawn to Bennett's shadow magic, I was sure. But why?

Was the suppressed part of Daisy reaching out for him, or was the Goddess simply striving to remain connected to a powerful witch?

A shiver ran down my spine. We needed to know more.

According to fairy lore, she was a dark witch and the Fae Goddess of Death associated with the crone aspect of the Morrigan. She was the deity the crone called on for her dark spells when alive, but we never truly researched Macha's origins, or more specifically, her intent.

What a stupid mistake.

Not that there was a lot of material readily available about a Death Goddess for just anyone to read. The stories and legends were just that—passed down from generation to generation. From one dark witch to another.

I swallowed hard, staring at Daisy's limp body through the cleansing haze, but hope remained. White magic always triumphed over dark. Of that, I was sure. We just needed to learn more, but until then, we had to trust in our magic and continue to do the best we could.

Still, the reaction she had to Bennett was something we couldn't ignore. Or at least something *I* couldn't ignore. There was a truth there, my own magic nudging me in that direction, and I would follow its pull the first chance I got. As soon as Daisy woke up and was safe again.

"Girls, gather 'round and repeat after me," Mom instructed.

Tightening our circle around Daisy again, we all listened and joined in, whispering the last part of Mom's spell together:

"Ties that bind, darkness entwined.
Release your hold on body and mind.
Free from evil shall you be.
Cleansed by light, so mote it be."

More of Macha's energy pooled on Daisy's skin, then evaporated into thin air. It seemed like a good thing, but suddenly I wasn't so sure.

The way it had altered my thoughts before—and how it had reached for Bennett—there seemed to be a sentience to Macha's energy, and I wondered if it was coalescing somewhere else, biding its time until it found another host. According to what little we knew, you had to open yourself up before it could take hold. Like when Daisy used the crone's spell to try to save me, or when I opened the bond between us when releasing her magic. Only then could Macha reach you.

I broke circle and ran for the nearest shelf. Upending the herbs from a glass jar, I picked up a knife on my way back to Daisy's side and quickly pricked her finger, holding it over the jar.

"What are you doing?" Fern screamed.

"It's not gone. Only waiting. We need to capture it."

"*It?*" Iris questioned.

"Yes. It! Macha's magic has a sentience to it, and we cannot let it go free."

With a drop of Daisy's blood now held within, I lifted the vessel above her body and summoned my full Fae powers.

"Darkness alive, you must abide.

Settle here, in the clear.

Bonded by blood, you'll seek no more.

Free from flesh, contained furthermore."

Black pools of dark energy sluiced through the air, slinking their way into the jar like snakes sliding through grass. I held the vessel aloft until it was completely full, then slammed the lid, sealing it shut.

I knew it.

Everyone gathered around me, peering into the inky goo. Bound in place by the drop of Daisy's blood, it had no reason to seek another host… for now.

I still had the urge to do more research about this ancient Goddess, especially why her magic was drawn to Bennett instead of one of us.

Daisy moaned, recapturing our attention.

"Oh, thank Goddess!" Mom cried out.

Easing onto her elbows, Daisy blinked up at us with wide eyes. "Is it done?"

I couldn't form words past the lump in my throat. Iris and Fern collapsed onto the pillows, pulling Daisy into one big hug, while Mom remained standing, wiping her eyes. But Aster stepped forward, grinding her smudge stick into an abalone shell and said, "It's done."

My oldest sister turned and laid a hand on my shoulder as she walked to the counter behind me. Picking up the discarded bundle of sage I left on the shelf, she snuffed it out, sharing a smile just with me.

With all that had been happening, I only now remembered about her and Craven, and another thought struck like lightning…

Craven also knew who Macha was, and perhaps now, he'd be more inclined to share.

Sixteen

Lily

With Daisy resting in the back of the shop under Mom's care, I pulled Aster aside. "I need to talk to you."

"Of course. Give me just a moment." Aster continued to clean up the remnants of our spell, disposing the ashes and loose bits of sage into the trash. "It was a good idea to trap Macha's energy in that jar. Well done."

I couldn't help my smile at her praise. It was still something I yearned for.

"Thank you."

Aster replaced the abalone shell on the shelf and gave the counter a quick wipe down before turning back to me. "Let's go for a walk."

I got the sense that she, too, had something she wanted to say. I hoped it was the revelation about her and Craven, or this might get awkward fast. I needed information, and unfortunately, that meant spilling the beans, whether she was ready to talk about it or not.

"There's something I've been meaning to tell you," Aster started. She kicked a pebble with the tip of her black ballet flat, acting most unlike herself.

I'd never known Aster to be shy or timid in any way, but I supposed the news of a secret entanglement with the leader of the Dark Elves might leave anyone tongue-tied.

"I already know," I blurted, hoping to put her out of her misery. "Craven stopped by the castle this morning and announced the good news."

Aster came to a dead stop in the middle of the street. "Oh, I see."

"Don't be upset. It was only Alder and me, and Alder already knew because of the negotiations."

"Negotiations?" Aster asked with a raised brow.

Oh, shit.

Until Craven had Alder's (and my) approval, he'd obviously refrained from informing Aster of his wishes just yet. She had no idea he was going to ask her to marry him, and now I was the one left tongue-tied.

"I'm so very happy for you," I gushed in a rush. "Does this mean you'll be staying in Ferindale permanently?" I walked on, hoping my redirection worked.

"Yes, I believe so. Especially with Mom and Hexx now here, there's no reason for me to return to Essex."

Thank goodness.

"That's wonderful news, Aster." I stopped and took her hand. "Having you all here means the world to me."

Aster returned my affection with a light squeeze, her pursed lips pulling up into a genuine smile. "I'm so glad." She sighed. "I know I've been hard on you, Lil. But it's only because I worry about you so much."

"I know. And it's okay." I nudged her shoulder, continuing down the brightly lit street.

White alabaster buildings glowed in the golden sunlight, sparkling like jewels against neon-colored clouds. Even the cobbled stones of the street and the exotic hanging flowers in the shops' windows glowed, as if fae magic infused it all.

I was so happy my family now called this home.

"So… when did this thing with Craven start?" I teased.

"Honestly, probably when he called me *ma'am* at our first meeting." She winked. "And it didn't hurt that he helped save our sister."

"No, I supposed it didn't." A boisterous laugh escaped me. I was so happy for my sister and Craven, and with Macha's influence now under wraps, all seemed to be right as rain.

I should have known better.

My darling, you are needed at home. Alder's thought penetrated my mind with a hint of urgency and fear.

"We must go." I tossed a portal ball on the ground and pulled Aster through the shimmering opening, emerging in the dining room of the Dartmoor castle, where Bennett's prone body thrashed against the black onyx floor. "What happened?" I rushed to his side.

Alder blocked me with his arm. "Keep your distance."

Staring down at my friend who was clearly in pain, and not being able to help wasn't going to work for me. "Please, tell me what happened!"

"You were right. Macha's dark magic *was* reaching out for Bennett at the shop. Clearly, it infected him before he was able to leave."

I gasped, fear clogging my throat.

"Wait," Aster spoke up, "I thought you had to *open yourself* via magic or spell in order to be affected."

I turned back to Alder, feeling his sorrow through our bond, and understood.

"He *was* open," I whispered. "His heart and mind were as open as can be when he saw Daisy in pain. His magic was reacting to his emotions subconsciously. I think it's probably something we've all experienced before."

I recalled the battle between Gideon and my father, when I thought my family was going to die. I'd embraced my destined role as Queen, but it was my inherent fae magic that burst forth at the idea of losing those I loved. A pure magical reaction without thought or direction, and the same thing must have happened to Bennett when he saw Daisy in pain. Overwhelmed by his care for her, he'd left himself wide open. Magically exposed. But for some reason, I still felt as though his shadow magic had more to do with this than anyone realized.

"Where's Craven?" I asked, earning looks from both Alder and Aster.

"Why?" Aster cocked her head.

"Because I think he has the answers I seek."

"Answers to what?" my husband asked.

"Why Macha's energy is so drawn to Bennett's dark magic."

Alder and Aster stared at me like I'd lost my mind, but I knew there was something there. Now, I just hoped Craven could help me reveal exactly what that might be.

Seventeen

Lily

Gretta kept watch over Bennett in the room across from ours, while Aster, Alder, Craven, and I sat around the dining room table, intently focused on our meal. Tension hung thick in the air, but whether from my lingering questions, Craven's desire to propose, or the simple fact that I'd never seen my sister act so reserved, I wasn't sure. Whatever the cause, it was grating on my nerves.

"So, can you think of any reason Macha's energy reached out for Bennett instead of one of us?" I motioned between Aster and myself.

Craven stabbed a piece of venison with his fork and seemed to savor the bite as he gathered his thoughts.

"I believe you're right, that it has something to do with his shadow magic. But to know for certain, you'd have to repeat the process in my presence," he eventually revealed.

Interesting.

Craven had been the first to sense Daisy was infected by Macha, and despite his willingness to answer my questions now, it still felt as if he was holding something back.

"That's never going to happen," Aster stated, and Craven knew it.

"Well, then, I suppose you'll just need to repeat the spell you used on Daisy to rid the lad of his ailment."

"His aliment?" I retorted.

Easy, darling. What's the matter? Alder reached under the table and laid a hand upon my knee.

I'm not sure why, but I think Craven knows more than he's letting on.

Alder lifted his head and straightened his shoulders, filling the room with his kingly presence. "If there's more you know, my friend, please share it with us now."

Goddess, I loved him.

Craven sputtered and coughed around the food in his mouth. "I... um... I'm afraid I cannot elaborate."

"And why is that?" Alder pressed.

Craven set down his fork and picked up his wine glass, taking a long pull. Meeting Alder's gaze he said, "Because I was sworn to secrecy a long time ago."

Lily

We spent the next hour trying to convince Craven to share his secret, but getting the Dark Elf to budge was almost as hard as the damn mountain under which he lived.

"Out of everyone, you should understand the constraints a leader must endure." He nodded respectfully to Alder and then me. "I cannot betray my people."

Aster walked forward and laid a firm hand on his shoulder. A slight shudder ran through the brute, and I had to stifle a laugh. Aster was a force, and I thought Craven was about to feel her effect.

"You said it yourself… we're amongst *leaders* and friends. If there's anyone you can trust, it's them." She leaned down and placed a kiss on his cheek. "And me." Sliding into the chair next to him, Aster never removed her hand.

Craven gave a firm nod and slammed his fist onto the table. The wood shuddered beneath the force, but the look in his eyes was soft and kind. "A very long time ago, the Dark Elves were sworn to secrecy when our magic failed against a powerful foe."

I gasped. "Macha."

"Yes. Hers is the only magic the stone from our mountain cannot subdue."

I looked down at my ring, honed from the same stone, and realized its limitations.

Oh, my Goddess. That's why he'd thrown Fern in the dungeon. At the time, without being sure whether she was the crone or not, he couldn't risk it when she started to call on Macha in her delirious state.

"How did you defeat her?" I asked.

Craven shook his head. "We didn't."

Everyone in the room gasped.

"When was this? What happened then?" Alder scooted forward in his chair. "And why is none of it in our history books?"

With downcast eyes, Craven continued. "It was long before you were born. Before your great-grandmother ruled the entire realm… back when Gods and Goddesses walked our lands and frequented our celebrations. When Macha decided she wanted it all for herself.

"Originally, Macha was associated with the land, fertility, war, and horses during her maiden and mother years. But as the Goddess aged and became the crone aspect of the Morrigan, she embraced her title of the Goddess of Death and laid claim to the land she'd personally blessed for so long.

"It was then that the citizens of the Fae realm banded together in an attempt to stop her. But Macha had killed her brethren, leaving her the only God or Goddess with access to our realm. And in her new form, the land began to die. Fields of green turned black overnight, and the brightly-colored clouds became gray and sullen, hanging over us with ominous intent. We had to do something, but none of our efforts worked against the Goddess... so we were forced to make a deal."

"You speak as if you were there," I interrupted.

"No. But my great-*great*-grandfather was. As the leaders of our people, we've carried this secret within our family for generations."

He lifted his chin, his jaw flexing, and a heavy uncomfortableness settled on his shoulders, driving home how sacred this information was.

"Thank you for sharing with us."

Craven reached for Aster's hand, gently cradling it in his own. "It seems now is the time. Our families will be intertwined soon enough, and this secret will become yours to bear as well."

I hadn't thought about that, and until we knew the end of the story, I wasn't going to.

Alder pulled me onto his lap and waved for Craven to continue.

"After it became clear we could not defeat her, a deal was struck that allowed Macha to be reborn unimpeded. She would cycle through her phases of the Triple Goddess again and again—Maiden, Mother, Crone—and in doing so, would continually nourish, grow, and destroy the world in an endless cycle of death and rebirth." He raised his head, meeting each of our gazes. "This is the second cycle of Macha in her crone form, and if you let it play out, she will soon become the maiden again, and all will be well for centuries to come."

Alder tensed beneath me, a low grumble reverberating through our bond. "You expect us to let her continue infecting those we love?"

"That is not my wish, my friend, but as this is my first time experiencing her in crone form, I'm not sure what to expect." Craven released Aster's hand and stood from the table. "When your great-grandmother, Gwenlyth Trelayne ruled the realm, Macha was still in her mother phase, nourishing the land with fertility and abundance, so there was nothing amiss to record in your history books."

I rose from Alder's lap and walked around the table to stand by our friend. "You said yourself that it is time. I think we *do* need to record all of this. All of what's happening during her crone phase—for future generations to come."

Craven hung his head, as if revealing this secret had broken something inside of him. "I understand the need, but please leave out the essence of our deal. That is for the leaders of the Dark Elves, and now the three of you, alone."

I glanced back at Alder, who nodded his agreement.

We both understood the consequences of being in charge and would not betray our friend. However, I was already thinking of ways to stop Macha once and for all. But that was a secret I'd keep to myself… for now.

Eighteen

Lily

Silver stars blazed beyond the glass roof of the dining hall as night fully enveloped Dartmoor. Servants gathered the plates and cleared the food from the table as we'd bid Craven and Aster goodnight.

I wasn't ready to go to bed just yet.

I leaned forward and rested my elbows on the table. "Do you believe Macha was drawn to Bennett's shadow magic because it comes from the Dark Elves?" I asked Alder. It was something I was still trying to puzzle out.

"I suppose so. Since all shifter and shadow magic originate from the Dark Elves, it stands to reason it would be easier for Macha to manipulate versus a witch's magic, since the magic of their mountain cannot affect her." Alder shrugged and stood from his chair, guiding me out of mine before wrapping his arms around me. "Can we think about this tomorrow?"

I nuzzled into his chest, welcoming his embrace. "Yes, I suppose we can." I spun in his arms and lifted my chin. "But you should know, I'm not giving up. I'll think of a way to stop Macha once and for all."

"I didn't doubt it for a second." Alder kissed my forehead and led me from the hall. He was right. This was something we could continue tomorrow, but first, I needed to check on Bennett and Daisy.

Gretta sat quietly next to Bennett's bed, wringing out a rag in the nearby bowl as I entered the room.

"How's he doing?" I whispered.

"Better. I believe the witch side of him is fighting against Macha's influence, and we should be able to extract it the same way you did for Daisy."

"That's good news. Thank you, Gretta."

She dipped her head and resumed her caretaking duties as Alder guided me across the hall.

I couldn't believe all that Craven had revealed. The notion we had no choice but to accept the Goddess's destructive phase nagged at me with clawing intent as I dressed for bed.

As soon as my head hit the pillow, I reached out through our sisterly bond and nudged the edge of Daisy's subconscious, checking to see if she was awake.

I'm here. And I'm fine. Your spell to trap Macha's energy with my blood worked, and I'm so very grateful.

My sister's sweet voice drifted through my mind, and my eyes welled with tears. *I'm so glad you're okay. I'm sorry we couldn't stay.*

A moment passed, then Daisy asked, *What's wrong?*

There was no hiding the stress I felt, or the shame that my initial reaction was to lie to my sister and tell her nothing was wrong.

I couldn't do it.

Please don't worry, but when Bennett came to check on you at the shop, he was infected by Macha before he could flee. For some reason, her energy was drawn to his shadow magic, but he's here with us now, and he's fine. Tomorrow, we'll do another spell to extract her presence from him as well. All will be fine.

The silence in my head left me hollow. I reached out to make sure our connection remained and gasped when a seething rage flooded our bond.

I'm going to kill that bitch.

I'd never felt or heard my sister in such a state.

Dais, please. Let Aster and I do the spell on Bennett tomorrow, then we can meet up and discuss what happens next.

I had no solid plans yet but knew whatever was to come would involve all my sisters' help.

Silence reigned for a heartbeat or two, then... *Fine. Please do whatever you can to help him and reach out if you need the rest of us to come.*

I will. Goodnight, sister.

Goodnight.

I rolled over in bed, yanking the covers with me. "Are you all right?" Alder asked, rolling to face my back.

I lay still, pulling the duvet up to my chin. "Yes, I think so. Considering."

"Considering what?"

I took a deep breath. "Considering we're now facing an undefeatable Goddess. Considering our friend lying across the hall infected with dark magic that reacts differently than anything we've ever dealt with so far. Considering my sister is marrying the leader of the Dark Elves. Considering I haven't fully processed the fact that Mom and Hexx are really here." I blew out an exasperated breath. "There's just so much happening at once, but overall, yes. I'm all right. Or at least I will be."

Alder snuggled close, wrapping his arm around my waist. "One step at a time, my love. One step at a time."

Indeed. What else could we do?

Daisy

Thanks to our bond, I noted the moment Lily drifted off to sleep. Rising from the bed, I dressed in haste. I couldn't stay here and let my sisters tend to Bennett without me.

We'd all been given a supply of portal balls to keep at the ready, and despite Lily's comforting instructions, I'd be using one now.

I scribbled a note to Fern and Iris, then tossed the silver ball onto the floor. The familiar onyx hall lay just beyond the portal, and I quickly stepped through.

Lily and Alder slept beyond the door to my left, and I knew they'd want to keep Bennett close by, so I crept up to the thick door directly across the hall.

Putting an ear to the wood, I listened carefully before pushing inside.

Bennett lay prone on the bed, his chest rising and falling in a steady rhythm. An empty chair sat next to him, with a bowl and rag abandoned on the table beside it. Hopefully, Gretta wouldn't be returning tonight.

I eased into the wooden chair and reached out for Bennett's hand. His skin was cool to the touch, which was at odds to what I expected.

I thought he'd be burning up with fever, struggling to fight Macha's influence like the infectious disease it was. But perhaps Lily was right. His shadow magic was a balm to the Goddess, and now she was happy to lay dormant in his veins.

The urge to wake him pulled at me, but with the thought of what he'd be facing tomorrow fresh in my mind, he'd need to rest as much as he could.

I released his hand and settled in the chair, present and ready to spring into action should the need arise. But Goddess, bless us, I hoped it didn't arise.

I hoped all would go as smoothly as Lily believed. Unfortunately, I couldn't convince myself that it would. Something about the way Macha's magic had been drawn to Bennett set my teeth on edge. And until I saw it leaving his body with my own eyes, I wouldn't believe any of us were free from her grip.

I guess only time would tell.

Nineteen

Lily

I woke to a familiar sound—Aster and Daisy arguing.

"What are you doing here?"

"I came to help my boyfriend."

"Oh, so he's *officially* your boyfriend now?"

"Yes, Aster. He's my boyfriend, and it's none of your business. What about you? Why are you here?"

And... that was my cue.

Pulling on my robe, I stuck my head out the door. "Hey! People are trying to sleep, here."

Daisy pushed past Aster and yanked me into the hall. "Look, I know you said you and Aster would perform the spell, but it just didn't feel right to not be here with Bennett." Daisy shrugged. "I need to be able to help him, Lil."

I nodded my head infinitesimally, still trying to wake up. "I understand." I looked to Aster, whose wary expression was an obvious plea to keep my mouth shut about her and Craven. Alder was right... that was her story to tell. "Let me get dressed, and I'll have Gretta bring up all we need."

My sisters agreed and broke to their separate corners—Daisy into Bennett's room, and Aster down the hall and stairs toward the dining room.

I crept back into my bedroom, trying not to wake Alder, but clearly, it was too late.

"Do we not even have time for breakfast?" My husband's groggy voice pulled a smile from my lips. One that only grew when he rolled over, exposing his tan torso all the way down to his sexy V'ed waist.

"Sorry, my love. Urgent witch business is afoot." I leaned down and gave him a kiss and giggled uncontrollably when he pulled me on top of him. "Stop. I have to go. Daisy and Aster are waiting for me."

The light touch of his hand split my robe and moved up to cup my breast. "Your sisters can wait."

I started to balk, when Alder sent, *Bennett is fine. Sleeping peacefully with Daisy at his side. Be with me, wife. For I'm in need of your tending, too.*

I melted into his embrace, falling for him all over again, as I did every single day.

Alder ran a finger across my cheek then lower along my neckline, finally dropping down to follow the curve of my collarbone. "You are so beautiful."

Love infused his words, piercing me straight through the heart.

I pulled up the hem of my robe and pushed Alder back on the bed, positioning myself atop his glorious frame. "*You're* beautiful." Running my hands along the smooth, hardness of his antlers, I pressed a fingertip to its point, almost drawing blood. "And deadly, too."

At times, I forgot what an imposing figure he truly was. To me, he was sweet, kind, loving, and always understanding. But to his men and everyone else in the realm, he was the Dark King—someone to be respected, and feared, if need be.

I traced a finger down his chest as I lowered myself onto him. Alder grabbed my hips, his fingers digging in as he pushed himself up, lifting his hips and his lips to mine simultaneously.

Together we fell, lost in one another as if it was our first time.

"Alder," I cried out, as his hands glided across my skin, touching me in his familiar way. The light streaming in from the window bathed our bodies in its soft morning glow while his touch remained firm and present. Peering down through my dark lashes, my eyes traced the outline of his face until the image became scorched into my being. I loved this man with all my heart. He was the air I breathed, the solid foundation on which I stood. And if I let him, he would carry me through anything we faced, good or bad, through thick and thin.

I love you, too, wife. More than my own life.

My heart pounded in my chest. "Alder." My voice came out huskier than usual as I met his gaze.

His eyes twinkled, and a slow grin curled his lips. Goddess, how I loved that smile. "Lily," he whispered my name on a ragged breath, and once again, we were all that existed in the world. Together as one—body, heart, and soul.

He shuddered beneath me, coming undone, and in turn became my undoing as well. With my powers barely contained, I rolled off his glorious body and curled up next to him, giving him a kiss.

He let out a hearty laugh. "I bet everyone's awake now."

Mortified, I smacked his chest and untangled my robe from our bodies. "Come on. Let's get dressed and go face everyone. We'll make time for breakfast, and then, it's time for my sisters and I to get to work."

Alder kissed me again before he climbed out of bed and walked into the bathroom, turning the shower on. "We'll be faster if you join me."

I couldn't resist his teasing smile and dropped my robe to the floor. "Fine, but we're only showering."

"Whatever you say, *Princess*."

I laughed at the old nickname he gave me when we first met and joined him under the warm water.

Twenty-minutes later, we met my sisters and Craven in the dining hall for breakfast.

Warm waffles, fresh fruit, and a variety of juices spanned the table.

"Ah! The love birds emerge from their nest." Craven's boisterous laugh softened the embarrassment a bit, but only slightly.

"Good morning, all," Alder offered casually, like they hadn't just heard us making love.

I took a seat and dug into my delicious breakfast without a word. Forks and spoons clanged against the china as my sisters followed suit. Finally, Aster spoke, breaking the silence.

"Daisy, you might as well know now, as we'll be sharing the news soon."

I jerked my head up, happy for the shift in subject to someone else's love life besides mine.

"Craven and I are… involved," Aster deadpanned, waiting for Daisy's response.

My gaze teetered between my sisters, the eldest stone-faced and the youngest in shock with her mouth hanging agape. Making the scene even more comical, Craven reached across the table to take Aster's hand.

The formality of these two was ridiculous to me, but I realized that's what made them perfect for each other.

"Alder and I are so happy for you both," I said sincerely, hoping to break the awkward tension hanging in the air.

Daisy shifted in her seat, gawking at me, but finally turned and offered her congratulations as well. "I'm sorry. I don't know what to say, except… what a wonderful surprise!" Rising from her chair, she rounded the table and draped herself around Aster's back with a genuine hug. "Does this mean you're staying in the fairy realm, too?"

Unpeeling herself from our sister's embrace, Aster nodded her head. "Yes. It's my plan to move to Glenmiere with Craven next week, since I recently accepted his proposal."

Twenty

Lily

My mouth hung agape; my fork frozen in midair. "You're moving in together next week? You haven't even told Iris or Fern that you're involved yet, or Mom that you're engaged."

"Yes, well, there have been other pressing matters to deal with, wouldn't you say?" Aster raised a brow, driving her point home.

She was right, of course, but the *little* sister in me hated to admit it.

"As much of a shock as this is, for once, I agree with Aster," Daisy added. "And a very important person to me is laying upstairs, waiting for us to help him right now."

"Of course, I'm sorry." I stood and motioned to Gretta, relaying all we'd need. "Please bring a sealable glass jar, three bundles of sage, and a knife up to Bennett's room."

Gretta nodded and shuffled off to gather our supplies.

"Let's finish breakfast, then we'll head up." I reclaimed my seat and waited for Daisy to do the same.

Lily

Ten minutes later, we stood over Bennett's bed with our lit smudge sticks in hand, whispering the same spell Mom used before. Instructing Daisy to hold open the jar, I reached for the knife.

"Wait! What are you going to do with that?" she balked.

I looked down at her finger, noting the small pinprick from where I'd gathered her blood. Of course, she didn't remember, being in the state she was in. "I had to prick your finger for a drop of blood in order for the spell to work."

She glanced down at her index finger and gasped. "Oh, I see."

I gave her a soft, reassuring nod, then reached for Bennett's hand.

I suppressed a shiver at the cold, clammy feel of his skin.

I thought that was odd, too, Daisy sent into my mind, obviously sensing the emotion I was trying to hide.

It'll be okay. Let's just get this done.

Aster stood at the end of the bed, waving her smudge stick over Bennett's legs and nodding she was ready.

Black dots of Macha's inky magic began to form on Bennett's skin, drawn out by the cleansing smoke. Unfortunately, it wasn't as much as I expected—like it was consciously fighting to stay inside him. I pricked his finger, transferring the blood with a tap of the knife to the side of the jar, then started the chant.

"Darkness alive, you must abide.

Settle here, in the clear.

Bonded by blood, you'll seek no more.

Free from flesh, contained furthermore."

Bennett screamed and black smoke erupted from his mouth, filling the room in a choking fog. I squinted and stared as the drop of blood in the jar slammed against the edges, as if alive and desperate to escape.

"Daisy, give me the jar and hold him down."

I felt the cool press of glass in my hand and moved closer to the bed, lifting the jar above Bennett's body.

"Darkness alive, you must abide.

Settle here, in the clear.

Bonded by blood, you'll seek no more.

Free from flesh, contained furthermore."

I yelled to my sisters, "Say it with me!"

Their voices joined mine as we tried again. But on the third attempt, Daisy's words sounded strange, and a horrible feeling settled in my gut.

"Daisy, are you okay?" I waved the thickening smoke away from me and gasped when I saw my sister's face.

Strained in fear, her hands, arms, and neck were covered in black goo.

"No!" I shouted, watching in horror as it crept up and into her mouth.

Bennett settled and stood from the bed, the smoke instantly clearing from the room. He, too, had black veins creeping up his neck and covering the side of his face.

This was a freaking nightmare.

"Lily, watch out!" Aster grabbed me by the shoulders and yanked me out the door as Bennett lunged forward.

With a sickening smile and odd, stiff movements, he reached for Daisy, tossed a portal ball onto the floor, and before Aster or I could move, disappeared inside with our infected sister in hand.

"No. No! This cannot be happening!" I stomped back into the room and threw the glass jar with all the strength I had.

Glass shattered across the floor, stained red with the tiniest drop of Bennett's blood.

"We have to go after them! We have to save them!" I shouted desperately, wracking my brain as to what a true queen would do. I fumbled for another portal within my skirt as Alder came running down the hall, urgently assessing the situation.

"What happened?" he demanded.

I could feel my mouth straining to move, but no words came out as I came up empty handed. I didn't have another portal ball with me and couldn't go after them.

Aster sniffled behind me and explained to Alder as calmly as she could. "Daisy was attempting to hold Bennett down during our spell, and in doing so, she was infected again."

I understood her words, but the only thing I could focus on was the shake in her voice. "They disappeared through a portal. They're gone, Alder. They're both gone."

My heart cracked open, spilling out nothing but grief and sorrow, leaving me hollow inside. I fell to the floor, collapsing into Alder's arms. "We have to go after them. We have to save them." This time, the words fell from my lips in barely a whisper. A silver light flared behind me, and Fern and Iris rushed into the hall.

"We felt Lily's distress. What's happened?" Iris demanded.

A strange ringing filled my ears, a piercing, glorious note that blocked everything out as Aster explained the situation again.

The weight of Alder's arm around me was the only thing holding me in place. If not for that, I would have floated away by now. Into the ether. Into the beyond where I could see and hear everything I needed to know that would bring this nightmare to an end.

My head lulled to the side as Alder lifted me into his arms. I was fading away, but before I closed my eyes, I saw a pair of tiny feet in delicate white shoes running toward us from down the hall.

White shoes.

An image of the library fire flared to life in my mind, scorching me with its memory. The presence of small white shoes and a piercing white light just before the fire went out shone brightly in my mind's eye.

"Gretta..." I whispered as Alder closed our bedroom door, plunging me into darkness again.

Twenty-One

Alder

"No, she's still despondent. Only waking long enough to roll over, adjust the blankets, and go back to sleep." I answered Aster's question, meeting her fierce gaze and admitting, "I simply don't know what else to do."

Lily's current state was understandable, but utterly terrifying in the fact that I couldn't even reach her through our bond. It was like she'd shut down her very essence, blocking out reality to avoid any more pain.

"Iris, Fern… go back to Ferindale and bring Mother here right away," Aster instructed.

The twins disappeared through another portal, straight into the main room of Hexx from what I could see. If anyone could reach Lily, it was Camellia… I hoped.

"What should we do about Bennett and Daisy?" Aster asked.

Her words sounded heavy due to the fog in my brain. With Lily lying distraught in our bed, I wasn't functioning as I should. "I, um… I suppose I'll have General Niasin and the Guard begin searching for them immediately," I offered with a clipped nod, then produced a portal of my own and stepped through without delay.

The neon-colored clouds of Ferindale seemed muted and dull, as if Macha's energy had already begun to sap their vibrancy. Pulling myself together, I strode to the practice arena and called out to the men. "Everyone, gather around."

A group of soldiers rushed into formation, standing before me in their precise, practiced lines.

"I come with alarming news." I straightened my shoulders and spoke as evenly as I could, tamping down how upset I truly was. "Bennett and Daisy have been infected by dark magic and have disappeared together." I lifted my chin. "We need your help to find them."

The crowd undulated, clearly distraught, but still focused and listening to what else I had to share.

"Be sure, this is not through any fault of their own. But we need to locate them right away, if we have any chance of saving them."

General Niasin strode to the front of the crowd and slapped a hand to my shoulder. "Just tell us what to do, my king."

I swallowed the emotion his dedication forced into my throat and instructed the crowd as one. "Start off by searching Bennett's home coven in Tamár, then check the other witch villages from there to the Lenorian Sea."

The men vocalized their "Yes, sir" as one, and split off to prepare. General Niasin turned to me, extended an arm in welcome, and walked with me toward his office.

The low stone building still sparkled in the daylight, but even its brilliant hue seemed more muted than usual.

"Any specifics I need to know, Sir?" he asked.

I sat in the leather, sling-back chair in front of his polished granite desk and shook my head. "Only to be on guard when you find them and send someone to notify me immediately. They are both infected with Macha's dark magic, and I'm not sure how they will react at this point." I held his gaze. "I don't want anyone to get hurt."

General Niasin was a good man and a terrific soldier, so I knew he understood. Bennett and Daisy were to be brought in peacefully, but there was also a chance they wouldn't come willingly. My hope was to portal Lily and myself directly to their location as soon as the Guard found them. And then, I hoped my queen and I would be able to talk them down, or at least subdue them long enough for her to recast the spell.

Rising from the chair, I thanked the General and tossed another portal ball onto the floor. Stepping back into the Dartmoor castle, I looked around my father's office and library and took a deep breath.

I needed a minute.

The rug was still singed along its edges from the fire Lily lit with her elemental power—influenced by Macha, of course, but the fact remained... This was serious, and there was a very real chance we could end up losing someone if we didn't figure out a way to stop the dark Goddess soon.

I couldn't fault Craven for the deal his ancestors made, but I hoped he wouldn't be opposed to us trying to find a different solution. One that would end the terror of Macha's crone phase forever.

Walking across the room, I ran a finger over the cover of my great-grandmother's book of shadows, back in its place on the altar. I hoped there was something inside that could help us achieve our goal, but I knew in my heart that only Lily would be able to find it. *If* I could coax her out of her current state.

The click of the door startled me, but I smiled as Gretta walked inside.

"Are you all right, Sir?"

"Yes. Just taking some time to think."

Gretta dipped her head, staring down at the charred edges of the large Persian rug on which she stood. "I think our queen is coming around and would benefit from your presence."

My head snapped up. "Lily's awake?"

I reached out through our bond, but still felt nothing.

"Any minute now, I'm sure." The corner of Gretta's lips curled up, and from years of experience, I knew she had a way of knowing things I did not."

"Thank you." I squeezed her shoulder as I rushed out the door then headed straight up the stairs to the bedroom hall.

The door to the room where Bennett and Daisy both previously resided stood wide open. A gaping reminder of the crisis we now faced. Twisting the gold handle of the door to my own room, I pushed inside with my heart in knots.

Lily lay in the same position as when I left her, but I believed Gretta was right. There was a different cadence to her breathing, like she teetered on the edge of just waking up.

A thought struck, and fear laced through my veins. What if she couldn't wake up? What if she'd tried to reach out to Daisy on her own and became ensnared in Macha's grasp again?

Oh, Gods.

I collapsed to the floor at the side of the bed, my knees and heart screaming in unison.

"Wait." Gretta's soft voice sounded behind me, and I stilled my hand. "Just give her a moment."

I heeded the words of my dear friend, wondering what she could feel or see that I could not. Then, in the next second, Lily woke up.

Blinking against the bands of sunlight filtering into the room, she rubbed her eyes and pushed herself up to lean against the headboard.

"Alder?" she whispered with a scratchy voice.

"I'm here, my love." Reaching for her hand, I rose from my knees and positioned myself on the side of the bed. "I'm so glad you're okay." I pressed my lips to the back of her hand, the heat of her skin a welcome balm to my frigid fears.

"I'm not okay. Or at least I won't be until we get Daisy and Bennett back." Her words were clear and full of steel now.

"I agree, and I've already sent General Niasin and the Guard to start looking for them."

Lily nodded, then looked up to meet Gretta's eyes. "I'm going to need your help now more than ever."

Gretta smiled, and bowed her head. "Of course, Your Majesty. Whatever you need."

II
Embers

Twenty-Two

Lily

Mom raced into the room, followed by Fern and Iris. "I came as quickly as I could. Are you all right?"

She took Alder's place on the side of the bed as he stepped away to talk to Gretta—something I, too, needed to do.

"I'm okay now, Mom. In fact, if you'll excuse me, I'd like to freshen up, then we'll meet you all downstairs for dinner, if that's all right."

My sisters nodded their heads with tears wobbling in their eyes. Mom pulled me into a quick, but stiff hug and whispered, "Take your time. We're not going anywhere." She stood from the bed and took both Fern and Iris by the hand. "Come on, girls, let's go find Aster. I think she has some news she'd like to share."

I smiled, happy that by dinnertime everyone would know of Craven and Aster's engagement. But in this moment, there was another secret I was keen to learn.

"I'll see you all later," I called out to my family as they left the room, then waved Alder and Gretta back inside.

Gretta pulled the desk chair in front of the couch as Alder and I took a seat. "I need to ask you something," I started.

"Of course." She bowed her head, ever the loyal servant.

"Do you have access to the Fairy Triad?"

Gretta smiled, a flush of relief shining in her eyes. "Yes, Your Majesty. It will take me but a day to gather them."

"Wonderful! After my self-induced commune with the Goddess, I believe they will make a difference in our stand against Macha."

"Would someone like to fill me in?" Alder asked.

"The Fairy Triad is a mixture of oak, ash, and hawthorn, used for centuries in the protection against fairies."

Confusion notched my husband's brow. "We are *all* fairies. Won't that have a negative effect on us?"

"Not in the way I plan to use it," I said confidently.

Alder shook his head. "All right. I trust you wife, but I think I need to know more about this *commune with the Goddess* you speak of."

I closed my eyes and took a deep breath. "My heart and magic were thrown off balance by the shock and grief of Bennett and Daisy's disappearance. I needed to go inside myself—and commune with *my* Goddess—as a way to regain that balance." I cupped his cheek. "I'm sorry I didn't have time to explain."

The gentleness and love radiating from his eyes told me he understood, but the distress emanating through our bond caused my heart to ache.

"I'm fine now. I promise." I leaned in and placed a kiss on his cheek, then turned back to Gretta and shared my plan with them both.

"I believe we can use the Fairy Triad to create a balm, of sorts—a ground up poultice we can physically place on Daisy and Bennett's skin—the protective properties should draw out Macha's influence, whether it wants to emerge or not."

"Won't that hurt Daisy and Bennett, too?" Alder asked.

"Possibly, but since neither are full Fae, I'm hoping the effects on them won't be too bad."

Bennett was a fairy, but with his Dark Elf shadow magic, and his witch side being the most prominent part of his genetic makeup, I knew he could withstand it. And Daisy... since she was only part Fae, the effects should be even less for her. At least, that was my hope. Either way, it was a risk I was willing to take.

"Gretta, gather the ingredients as fast as you can. I'll have Mom, and my sisters help create the poultice, and then, as soon as we find Bennett and Daisy, we'll portal directly to them and save our family."

Gretta bowed again, then set off on her task. I wasn't sure whether she kept a secret stash of sacred ingredients hidden somewhere in her personal things, or if she'd need to forage the surrounding forests, but I knew I could trust her to obtain what we'd need. In fact, I knew she would play a pertinent part in defeating Macha, thanks to the vision I'd received from the Goddess.

There was more to Gretta's story, I was sure, but as Alder put it, it was *her* story to tell. And in time, I knew she would.

Lily

Mom, Aster, Fern, and Iris joined me in my new workspace in Dartmoor—an onyx-tiled, stone-wall space at the top of the castle—the following morning, ready to help. They agreed with my plan, and as I stared out the large stained-glass window towards the rolling hills of Ferindale, I pictured Alder finding Bennett and Daisy, safe and sound. But with the dull sensation running through our bond, I didn't think that was the case.

Alder had left over two hours ago to check his troops' progress but hadn't returned yet. I couldn't imagine that was good news.

"All set here, Lil. We just need the ingredients from Gretta, and we'll be good to go." Mom smiled, but it didn't reach her eyes.

I had already apologized for casting the spell on Bennett without her help, and she'd assured me, there was nothing additional she could have done if present. But after losing Gideon, learning of Fern's and my recent ordeal, and now having Daisy infected and missing, I wasn't sure she'd forgive me right away. In fact, I wasn't sure how long she'd stay in Ferindale, given the stress she had already endured.

"Thank you for being here. It means so much." Tears welled in my eyes. "After everything that's happened, I never thought we'd get the chance to do magic together again. And while I know it's not under the best circumstances, I'm still grateful to have you with me."

A sad smile bloomed on Mom's lips "Of course, honey." She pulled me into a hug. "There's nowhere else I'd rather be."

In that moment, I thought about Sybil—the leader of the Acrucian Coven, the killer of the crone, and Mom's dear friend. "I wish Sybil could be here, too," I shared out loud.

Mom tilted her head. "Why couldn't she be? She's either guarding her portal or ours, so with one quick message, she could easily join us here."

Mom was right, but was I only missing the powerful witch because of my sentimentality, or was the Goddess hinting to me that we'd need her to achieve our goal? Either way, the addition of her magic couldn't hurt. "Okay, do it. Send Sybil a message to join us, and I'll check with Alder again."

Mom retrieved a scrap of paper and a pen from the side cupboard along the far wall, then quickly scribbled a note to her friend. I tossed a portal ball onto the floor, mesmerized by its green swirling hue, and gave thanks they connected us to exactly where we needed to go. With only a thought, we controlled their destinations—a safeguard Alder and I put in place with our combined magic soon after I became Queen.

My eyes snapped up, taking in everyone in the room.

Aster, Fern, and Iris had tried to follow Bennett and Daisy after they disappeared but were unsuccessful, and now I understood why. It was due to Macha's influence.

While her magic and essence were real, she wasn't corporeal yet. Which meant, as long as Bennett and Daisy carried her tainted energy, we wouldn't be able to pinpoint them with our portals alone.

Alder's soldiers would *have* to find them first, or *we'd* have to figure out exactly where Macha needed to go.

Twenty-Three

Lily

As soon as Sybil joined us and Alder returned, I relayed my theory. "I believe if we figure out where Macha would want to go, we'll locate Daisy and Bennett there."

A low murmur of agreement rolled through our small group.

"And does anyone have an idea of where that might be?" Sybil asked. The High Priestess's violet eyes shone brightly with steeled intent, and I was so grateful she was here. Unfortunately, I didn't have an answer to her question.

"Craven might," Aster offered from a shadowed corner across the room. Stepping into the light, she added, "My fiancé has the most history with Macha, and I'm sure he might have an idea of where she would want to go."

"Yes," Alder agreed, nodding to Gretta. "I believe Craven is still in the dining hall. Please ask him to join us."

Gretta disappeared out the thick wooden door, returning with Craven in tow only a few moments later.

Joining his fiancée, Craven and Aster walked hand in hand toward the window. The Dark Elf peered north, and I immediately knew what he was going to say—Aster's long muted-gray dress should have been hint enough, for it was the exact same color as his mountain back home.

"I believe the Death Goddess has returned to Glenmiere. For it's where she is most powerful, and unhindered by the magic of our sacred mountain."

Of course! I should have thought of that before.

I joined my sister and friend in front of the large bank of windows and looked toward Glenmiere. A black cloud hovered in that direction, and for me, that was indication enough that the leader of the Dark Elves was right. Macha had returned to the mountain where she'd struck her original deal, ready to complete her crone phase again—but this time, it would destroy everything I loved.

Lightning struck, and I spun around, frantic with an idea. "What if we could stop her from completing her crone phase? Somehow force her beyond it, so she would be reborn as the maiden again?"

Wide eyes contemplated my wild idea, followed by triumphant, almost sinister grins.

"I think you might be onto something, my dear," Mom smiled. A confident, genuine smile that this time reached her eyes.

A flurry of activity erupted in my workspace. Ingredients were pulled from drawers and cupboards, tossed into wood, stone, and ceramic mortars, while thick books with ink-stained pages were pulled from the shelves.

Sybil joined Fern and Iris at the table in the center of the room. "Let's look through these quickly, and see if there's anything of value we can use to create a new spell."

Mom, Aster, and I carefully focused on creating the poultice with the ingredients Gretta had provided, while she, Alder, and Craven went to prepare our travel gear.

Without knowing Macha's true whereabouts, we simply couldn't portal in. Instead, we'd be heading north on horseback again.

A shiver ran down my spine.

Our last trip to Glenmiere wasn't something I wanted to be reminded of. Kidnapped, thrown in a dungeon, learning about my best friend's lie... it was the place Daisy had first called to Macha in her effort to save me—the true reason we were all here.

Fern and Iris looked up from the table, and a wave of affection filtered down our bond. They could sense my distress, and once again, I was so grateful for their presence and our sisterly connection.

"All done," Mom called out.

The mixture of ash, oak, and hawthorn—with the addition of marigold, tormenti root, and yarrow to aid in extracting Macha's poison—created a deep green poultice that Mom divided into three glass jars. With the lids sealed tight, she handed one to me and one to Aster, keeping the third for herself.

Sybil and the twins continued to scour the books, looking for anything that could help hasten a Goddess's life cycle, but after another hour, it was clear nothing of the sort existed.

I debated looking through Gwenlyth Trelayne's fairy handbook to spells and salvation again, but knew I'd find nothing there. Macha's deal was struck before Gwenlyth's time, so as Craven had explained, there was no history to be recorded—something I was still determined to change.

"Gretta, if you could prepare an early dinner, I think we all need to eat and get some sleep before traveling tomorrow."

Sybil's head snapped up from yet another book in her hand, sending waves of her red hair flying. "We're leaving tomorrow? Without a spell prepared?"

The knot that seemed to be permanently lodged in my gut tightened, but the rightness of what needed to be done sat firmly in my heart. "Yes. I have full faith the Goddess will show me the way and reveal what needs to be done."

Gretta disappeared from the room, followed by the twins, Aster and Craven, and finally my mom and Sybil, leaving only Alder and me standing side-by-side at the worktable.

"Are you sure departing so soon is a good idea?" he asked once we were alone.

"No, but I believe what I said. The Goddess will show me the way. Besides, more importantly, I know we need to get to Daisy and Bennett soon and administer the poultice, or we'll lose our chance to save them altogether." I looked up into Alder's caring eyes. "I feel it in my bones."

Leaning down, he placed a gentle kiss on my lips. "I do not doubt you, wife. Just tell me how else you think we should prepare."

I looked down at the desk, noting the paper and pen. "I need a bit of time alone before dinner. There's something I have to do."

Nodding, he kissed me again, and left me to get started on my own book of shadows—a record of all I learned and faced since becoming Queen.

I flicked my wrist and lit every candle in the room.

Twenty-Four

Lily

Page after page poured out of me as I scribbled my history into existence. Starting with my false childhood as a simple witch, protecting the Fae portals as part of my *familial* duty, to discovering my true identity and claiming my throne as queen of the entire realm… I wrote intricate spells and sketched drawings of vines and butterflies entangled with words that created a new story of their own. I depicted the essence of my true Fae magic, and how it lived inside me, and notated the shadow and shifter magic that originated from the Dark Elves. I recorded all that we now knew about Macha, heeding Craven's request to leave out the deal his ancestors made.

As midnight approached, I searched the cupboards for the perfect cover and bindings to complete my book, and on the top shelf I found two thick cover boards and a spool of black leather cord covered in dust.

When my fingers glided over the items, I knew they were what I needed.

Spreading out my materials on the table, I grabbed a cloth to clean the cover, and gasped at what my efforts revealed.

Inlaid into the dark leather-wrapped board was a gold crown with a vibrant flame burning inside.

I quickly gathered my freshly scribed pages and stacked them between the two covers. Then, using the hole punch I found in a drawer, I pushed it through the layers of leather and paper and wove the leather cord up through the holes I'd made to create the spine.

It was rudimentary, but as soon as I laid down my tools and cracked the cover, a bright golden light burst from within.

Transformed into a thick sealed tome, my book of shadows came to life. Secured beneath three golden locks, the flaming crown on the cover now shimmered in the dim light of my altar room, and I felt our future settle into place.

"*Of essence and embers,*" the Goddess's words floated to my mind.

"Yes. That's it." I could feel the rightness in my soul.

This Queen's handbook to essence and embers would serve as a record for generations to come, sharing what could be accomplished through will, trust, and love.

A knock sounded at the door, followed by Alder's deep voice. "I brought you some food, my love. Is it all right if I enter?"

"Of course. Why would you even ask?" I looked up and smiled at the sight of my husband carrying a silver platter filled with food.

"Because I could sense your magic flaring for the last few hours and didn't want to interrupt."

"Really? I hadn't realized I'd been using my magic at all."

"Yes. I could tell whatever you were working on was important." He set down the tray and gasped when he saw the book. "Oh, Lily. It's beautiful."

Suddenly shy for reasons unknown, my cheeks flushed as I lifted the book from the table. "My own book of shadows. Or as I like to call it, my handbook to essence and embers." I handed it to my husband, smiling proudly. "It contains everything that's happened to me, and all the specifics about the essence of my inherent Fae magic as well as the elemental gifts my sisters and I were bestowed when Gideon's prophecy was fulfilled. Everything we've learned about Macha," I lifted my chin. "*and* how we plan to stop her."

"You've worked out the spell?"

"Yes, I believe I have."

Lily

After a short, but good night's sleep, I pulled on my dark brown, fleece-lined leggings, my thickest cream cable-knit sweater, and my black riding boots. I hadn't been to the stables since the last time we rode home from Glenmiere, but I was excited to see Luna again, and the beautiful white mare seemed just as excited to see me.

"Hi, girl. I'm sorry it's been so long." Retrieving an apple from the basket near the stall door, I offered her my apology in food form and began to saddle up.

Alder sat astride Samson, his favorite black stallion, while Craven pulled Aster in front of him atop his regal buckskin steed. The stable master had prepared mounts for each of my sisters, but Fern and Iris chose to ride together on Soven—the horse that previously carried Bennett.

Mom and Sybil each mounted their own horses, a pair of beautiful chestnut mares.

At Alder's request, General Niasin had also joined us on his large, gray-dappled horse, along with a handful of men, including Dylan, who had accompanied him to Glenmiere before.

We were all mounted and ready to go, when Craven called out to the group. "Allow me to take the lead. For I will know when something is amiss."

Each of us nodded our agreement, then fell in line as we set off to the Dark Elves' stronghold in the north.

Sliding up beside me as quiet as a shadow, Gretta surprised me with a wink as she guided her silver mare into step beside Luna. "I know when I'm needed," was all she said.

I smiled and returned my focus to the road, enjoying the journey into the mountains as much as I could as the temperature continued to fall.

The landscape remained the same as before—a speckled forest full of evergreen trees and delicate frost-covered flowers scattered across the snow-ladened forest floor. It was beautiful. Peaceful. Yet contained so many frightening memories for me.

I glanced ahead at Craven's wide back, remembering being thrown over his broad shoulders and carried into these exact woods.

A shiver ran through me but was suddenly replaced with a warmth radiating up my legs. I looked down to see Alder's hand on my boot near my knee. "Are you all right, my dear?"

I sent a wave of love between us, silently thanking him for his vigilant concern. *Yes. I was lost in my previous memories of Craven and didn't realize it was something I still needed to process.*

I understand, and I am so sorry for what you went through. Alder's thoughts carried the usual guilt about what happened, but he knew I didn't blame him. I didn't really blame Craven either. Everything that happened was the crone's fault at the time, but it seemed some trauma remained.

I'm okay, I sent to my husband, forcing myself to believe it, too.

Shifting the backpack strapped over my shoulders, I drew strength from the weight of my book of shadows packed within. When preparing to leave, the urge to take it with me was overwhelming, and I'd learned not to ignore feelings like that.

The Goddess was guiding me now more than ever.

Gretta reached in my direction from atop her silver mare. "Here, my lady. Drink this. It will help ease your chill." She handed me the cup from her thermos, full of warm frothy liquid which I downed immediately.

"Thank you, my friend. That's exactly what I needed."

Twenty-Five

Lily

A half-day's ride later, we made camp in a new spot alongside the main road. I instinctively knew Alder had told General Niasin to pick somewhere different than before, and I couldn't be more grateful.

The soldiers of the Guard quickly went to work erecting our camp. Raising tents for everyone in pairs.

Alder and I were in the royal tent, of course, with Craven and Aster's tent directly beside us. Fern and Iris, Mom and Sybil, and an individual tent for Gretta was placed in a half circle in front of us, with the Guard's quarters and General Niasin's filling in the front line of defense.

Craven and Alder agreed that we were safe here, and I doubted very much that Macha would leave her stronghold to venture into the woods to attack us here. But still…

"Come here, my love. Let me hold you close." Alder pulled my back to his chest, wrapping his arm around my middle. "There, that's better."

I closed my eyes and focused on my breath, trying not to breathe too deeply. A steady rhythm in and out grounded me as I worked to center myself.

Alder used his elemental power to warm every aspect of our tent, so the chill I felt wasn't from the cold.

I knew our plan would work, but there were so many unknowns that left me on edge.

First, we had to locate Bennett and Daisy, then get close enough to smear them with the poultice containing the Fairy Triad. After that, I had no idea what would happen, but I assumed once Macha's energy was drawn out of her last remaining hosts, she may choose to then show herself as Craven indicated she used to do. In her true Goddess form, walking our realm in her crone phase, the devastation to our land would set in immediately, of that I was sure.

"I know you're focused on what we have to do, but please, Lily, calm your mind. You need to rest if we have any hopes of pulling this off." Alder kissed my head, nuzzling my hair and shifting in the bed to settle himself perfectly around my curves.

He was right. I needed to rest, but I couldn't shut off my brain. Thankfully, the steady rise and fall of his chest against my back as he slipped into the oblivion of sleep helped me to do the same.

A crack split the cobblestone path, spreading like a sinking canyon carving its way across the surface of the land. Dark energy crept out like insidious vines intent on choking the joy from our world. It was the vision from Macha all over again, only now it made sense.

The sky darkened, and all the surrounding trees dropped their magically blackened leaves, blanketing the ground to look like a living, breathing pit of despair. The tree branches turned to spindly fingers and stretched threateningly in my direction.

"Wake up. Wake up," I whispered to my dreaming self.

More darkness spewed out every few seconds like belching lava, and same as before, my chest tightened and matched its sinister beat.

Thankfully, like last time, I cast my eyes to the sky and embraced the moonlight as it fought its way through Macha's devastation. Silver light sliced through black, thunderous clouds, highlighting the peak of the all-too-familiar mountain in front of me.

Glenmiere.

Macha *had* returned to the Dark Elf stronghold, and with her power unchecked, we may already be too late. She was nearing the peak of her crone phase, and things were only going to get worse. Very soon, she would have the ability to ruin the entire realm again.

A howl on the wind woke me, freeing me from the reality of my nightmare.

"It's okay, my love. It's only some wolven passing by."

Since my first foray into the woods, I'd learned of the many creatures that roamed our land. The packs of wolven—shifters that turned from man to wolf. The moonbiens of Devonshire—pure-white, silver shining unicorns. The embertines of Halcion—firedrakes that lived far to the south. And of course, all classes of sprites and fae, and the morphineas that roamed freely across our land.

Our world was a melting pot of magical beings, and I was proud to be their queen.

Now, I just had to figure out how to save us all.

The spell that came to me while creating my book of shadows was only the beginning. I knew in my heart it would take everyone working together to stop the Fae Goddess of Death.

More howls rang out in the night, and I curled into my husband's chest. A sense of foreboding overtook me, and I began to shake beneath the blankets.

"Honey, it's all right. They won't attack us here."

I wanted to believe him, but the image of ink-dipped paws and black stained teeth flashed into my mind. "I wouldn't be so sure about that. I think they've been infected by Macha's dark magic."

Alder sprang from the bed, not hesitating or second-guessing me for a moment. "Stay here. Do not leave this tent, do you understand me?" He held my face between his palm, barely giving me room to nod in agreement, then kissed me hard and disappeared into the night.

If my vision was true, things were much worse than we thought. When Daisy and Bennett were the only two infected, we had a chance to use the poultice to free them. But if others had been tainted as well, our plan would fail, and at that point, I wasn't sure what we were going to do.

Howls turned to growls right outside our camp, followed by grunts and shouts as Alder directed his men.

I shrank further beneath the blankets, wondering if Mom and my sisters were doing the same. But after a few moments of silence, I crept to the opening of our tent and peeked out the flap, hoping to get an idea of what was happening outside. Craven and Aster's tent was close enough I could see candlelight shining from within. So with a silent apology, I broke my promise to stay put and ran for my sister's tent.

I crashed through the opening, calling out her name. "Aster!"

"Lily! What's happening? Are you okay? Where did the men go?"

Craven had joined Alder, leaving her alone. Not that I expected differently, but for some reason, I hoped the Dark Elf had stayed behind. "I believe the wolven in the area have been infected by Macha, and the men have gone to…"

Aster grabbed me by the shoulders when the words stalled on my tongue. "Gone to what? Kill them? Chase them off? What, Lily?"

It was then I realized I had no idea how they would defeat this threat. Especially if the tainted beasts were hunting in a pack.

"We have to help them!" I shouted.

I ran back toward the opening of the tent and tossed Aster her coat and boots. "Without our magic, they don't stand a chance. Craven's staff won't work against Macha's magic, and I don't know how many infected wolven there are."

Twenty-Six

Lily

By the time Aster and I arrived at the battle, our efforts were no longer needed. A row of six dark brown wolven with their fur covered in a layer of black goo, lay sprawled out on the snow-covered forest floor. They were tied down in the clearing by a thick twist of roots, while Fern, Iris, Mom, and Sybil stood off to the side under a canopy of nearby trees. Iris dipped her head, confirming what I saw.

They, too, had come to the same conclusion and rushed to aid the men with their magic. She had subdued the wolven using her earth element, and I couldn't be prouder.

"Is this all of them," I asked, my eyes frantically scanning the forest for more.

Alder emerged from between the evergreens before anyone could answer, his antlers gleaming in the moonlight and casting an impressive shadow across our newly-created foe. "How did you come to be here? How did you become infected with this muck?" His voice was that of the King, deep, dangerous, and full of power.

The wolven squirmed beneath the roots, snapping their powerful jaws and struggling to free themselves and escape the wrath of the men now surrounding them.

Craven stood with crossed arms over his burly chest, while General Niasin and the Guard took up posts along the edge of the trees. Alder paced in front of the wolven's bloodied snouts, ignoring their snarls and snaps as he evaluated his next move.

One of the creatures seemed less violent, a light tan wolf with swirling green eyes. I sent a nudge to Alder down our bond.

Approaching that particular wolf, he nodded to Iris, who gently released the root ensnaring his snout.

"I'll ask only once more. How did you become infected and sent here?"

The other wolven snarled in unison—a warning to their brother not to talk. But when Alder slammed down the tip of his sword in front of the wolf's face, talk he did.

He spoke like a man, though still in wolf form. "We were hunting nearby a few days ago, when a woman and man appeared along the trail. As you know, fairies aren't our usual prey, but there was something about them that called to us. As soon as they spotted us, the woman screamed, and a cloud of black fog erupted from her mouth."

I gasped, and all the wolvens' eyes snapped toward me.

He paused to squirm against the roots still entwining his body. "When we woke, our bodies were covered with this black goo, and our only desire was to find and stop you."

There was little doubt he was describing Daisy and Bennett, but I had to be sure.

I took a step forward, cautiously nearing Alder's position in front of the wolf. "Did the man have light spiky hair, and the woman long chestnut locks?"

"Yes," the wolf answered through black bared teeth.

Goddess, no. How was Macha's infection of Daisy so much worse this time around?

I'd tried to reach her so many times since she disappeared. But every effort left me exhausted and heartbroken—our connection nothing but a silent, hollow void.

Aster called out from behind us, joining the conversation. "How did you know where to find us?"

Again, the wolven growled in unison, and this time the lone wolf cowered beneath their will.

Stepping closer, Aster demanded, "Tell me now, wolf, or the king's sword will be the least of your concerns." Fury radiated from my sister's voice, and the sting of her building magic snapped against my skin.

I saw movement to our left in my mind's eye, but my reaction to warn anyone was a second too late.

The wolf next to the cowered one broke the roots around his nose and sank his black teeth into Aster's ankle before any of us could move.

Aster screamed, and Craven's staff came down with a crack against the wolf's head.

Gathering her in his arms, Craven cradled Aster against his chest, whispering affirmations that all would be okay.

I wiped away the building tears in my eyes as the Dark Elf carried my sister back toward camp, safely in his arms. Fury reigned as the rest of my family and Sybil unleashed their magic on the pack, and in a matter of moments, it was over.

Six carcasses lay dead, either strangled by Iris's roots, frozen and shattered by Fern's water, or fried and charred to a crisp by Mom and Sybil's combined efforts.

Alder and I didn't have to do a thing.

"Let's get back to camp, I have to check on Aster." I turned away from the gruesome scene, the crunch of snow filling my ears as tears ran down my cheeks.

Alder took my hand, adding his warmth to mine own. "It couldn't be helped, Lil. There was no saving them."

I shook my head and let the tears fall—my sobs melding with those of my family who shuffled behind us through the snow.

Never had my family used their magic for such a purpose, and I could feel deep it my bones that what just transpired was going to leave a scar on us all.

As we neared our royal tent, I nudged Alder toward Aster and Craven's instead, desperate to check on my sister's state. I reached for the opening, but thought better of simply barging in. "Aster, Craven, may Alder and I come in?" I called out.

Soft sobs were stifled, and I imagined Aster putting on her usual stoic armor, then Craven opened the flap. He invited us in with a nod of his head, and I ran straight to Aster's side, falling to my knees.

"Are you all right?" I took her hand, looking for any signs of Macha's taint.

Aster cleared her throat. "I'm fine. In fact…" She swiped the blankets back, revealing her injured leg, and I gasped in shock. "Besides the residual pain, I'm completely fine." Two punctures marked where the wolf had sunk in his teeth, but beyond a small smear of blood from them cleaning the wound, her leg was completely normal.

"How?" I gawked between Aster, Craven, and Alder, hoping someone could provide an answer that made sense. There was no evidence of Macha's black magic, only smooth skin, and I desperately needed to know why.

Aster looked to Craven and nodded, deferring all the attention to him.

The Dark Elf took a deep breath, enlarging his chest even beyond its usual girth. "We believe it's because she's fully human. The Goddess of Death can only infect the Fae."

Twenty-Seven

Lily

Craven's explanation sent me fully to the floor. I sprawled beside my sister's bed, still clasping her hand as it dangled over the side.

"Lil, this is a good thing. I'm not infected at all." She swung her legs over the bed and peered down at me through a curtain of her corn-silk hair. "We just need to figure out how to use this against her."

Use it against her? We were in the fairy realm, for goodness' sake, an entire world filled with beings that would fall prey to Macha's energy soon enough. Not to mention, I had no idea if the wolven's bite would illicit some other complication—we hadn't gotten that far yet.

"I don't see how that's possible," I admitted, defeat sinking me further into the ground.

Aster scooted off the bed and sat beside me on the cold canvas floor. "I think between all the powerful witches and Fae royalty here, we'll be able to figure something out." She nudged me with her shoulder.

Perhaps she was right. Perhaps I wasn't seeing this as the potential gift it was, but at present, I couldn't puzzle out how we could use my sister's humanity to our advantage.

"I think we all need to get some sleep," Alder stated, interrupting my spiraling thoughts. "Then, tomorrow morning, we can discuss this as a family and come up with a plan."

Craven grumbled his agreement and helped Aster off the floor and back into bed.

Alder's kind eyes met mine, and I happily accepted his outstretched hand. "You're right, of course." I pulled my sister into a tight hug before leaving. "I'm so glad you're okay."

She squeezed me back, releasing me as a stray tear ran down her cheek. "Me, too."

Alder and I emerged from the tent to find Mom, Sybil, and my sisters hovering outside.

"We were coming to check on Aster when we heard the four of you and didn't want to interrupt." Mom pulled me into a hug of her own. "We'll figure this out. I promise."

In that moment, I was eight years old all over again. Cradled in my mother's arms, crying about something I had no control over, and praying to the Goddess that she was right—that we would figure out something to solve the dilemma we were facing and magically solve all my problems again.

Releasing me, Mom, along with Sybil and my sisters, returned to their respective tents, and I followed Alder to ours. "Thank you for everything you've done for my family," I blurted out, grateful we were all together and allowed to call this realm our home.

Alder followed me to our bed, tucked me beneath the blankets, and fiercely held my stare. "Why are you thanking me for something you wholly deserve? Your family is here because *you* are the rightful queen of this realm, not because I will it so." He ran a hand down my disheveled hair. "The fire within you burns as brightly as your red locks, and with your powers now under control, I know we will stop Macha once and for all. Together."

Love, confidence, and utter commitment shivered down our bond. He truly did mean every word he said.

"Thank you for believing in me. Especially, when I do not." I reprimanded myself internally. I'd been doing so well, embracing my Fae essence and believing in myself and my decisions as Queen. But when faced with the fear of my family being hurt, I'd become a shrinking flower again.

"We are the flower girls, and proud of it!" The thought drifted into my mind, sent from Iris and Fern who couldn't help but feel all my emotions as they were laid bare.

"Thank you for being here, too. I couldn't do this without either of you," I sent back.

Again, feelings of love, determination, and acceptance shivered into my mind as I closed my eyes. They were all right… we would figure this out. Together.

Lily

Morning came, and snow glistened as far as the eye could see when I opened our tent and welcomed everyone inside.

Gretta had miraculously prepared a delicious spread of bagels, lox, and cream cheese, fresh fruit, and what seemed to be an endless supply of coffee, which I desperately needed.

Gathered around the small desk that served as a table, we each made a plate then found a spot to sit and began to nibble on our food.

No one spoke as we enjoyed the light fare, but the tension in the room was building by the minute.

Aster finished first and sat her plate on the floor by her feet. "If you all heard our assumptions last night, you know Craven and I believe that I'm immune to Macha's influence because I'm not Fae, and we'd like to get your thoughts."

Iris and Fern nodded simultaneously and continued chewing, while Mom placed her plate carefully in her lap. "I can only hope you're right. Because if that stands to reason, then Sybil and I would be immune, too."

I chastised myself again. *Why hadn't I thought of that?* There had to be something there we could use against Macha, but I was still unsure as to what.

"How does that help us?" Iris asked, voicing my very thoughts.

"I'm not sure that it does, besides keeping us free from influence when it matters most," Mom responded.

What *did* matter most? Stopping Macha from completing her crone phase, or saving Bennett and Daisy?

"I think we need to continue onto Glenmiere and find Bennett and Daisy as soon as possible," I added. "If Macha is using them to infect others, freeing them with the poultice is still our best bet."

Heads bobbed around the room, but there was a hesitation in everyone's response.

"What? What is it? If you can think of a better plan, please speak up." I steadied myself for everyone's input, but sank into my chair when Alder finally spoke.

"I believe the safest thing we can do now is to send your mother and Aster into Glenmiere alone. If they are truly immune, they're the only ones who will be able to get close enough to administer the poultice and perform the spell." He turned to Sybil. "I cannot speak for you, as you are not a member of my realm, but I believe I know your heart, and you're welcome to join us too."

A heavy silence settled within the tent, suffocating me like a pillow being placed over my face. I took a deep breath but struggled to breathe. I was being pulled under again by panic and fear, but forced myself to hold Mom's gaze before I was yanked into oblivion again.

Twenty-Eight

Lily

Mom's wide eyes were the last thing I saw before I was pulled into the darkness. I braced for the worst but felt my body ease as images of Macha in her maiden form floated into my mind. Guided by the connection to *my* Goddess, I bore witness to how everything could play out, if only we were brave enough to see it through.

I woke up in the bed of our tent, surrounded by Alder, Gretta, Sybil, and Mom.

"I'm okay," I offered quickly. "Apparently, the Goddess wanted to share her vision of how we can defeat Macha." I sat up and rolled my neck. "I know what we need to do, but it's not going to be easy."

"Nothing worthwhile ever is," Mom commented, not understanding how this would affect her directly. Her *and* Aster.

"Apparently, you were right," I looked to my husband. "Mom and Aster have to do this alone." Sybil reached for my mom's hand, and I shook my head, forcing back my rising tears. "Since they are both now citizens of our fairy realm, yet fully-human and immune to Macha's influence, they are the only witches who can draw out her magic and contain it within."

"What do you mean, contain it within?" Sybil asked, her violet eyes shining with tears of their own.

"If Mom and Aster can siphon off Macha's magic while she's still in her crone phase, she'll transform into the maiden again and be trapped forever, unable to complete another cycle without her magic. But…"

Mom stepped forward. "But her magic needs to be contained in a vessel, just like the glass jar you used with Daisy."

I nodded my head, unable to hold back my tears any longer. "I'm sorry. I thought as Queen I could use my essence and burn Macha to dust, but the Goddess showed me it wouldn't work, and reminded me… *A Queen will always do as she must.* I just didn't realize that meant sacrificing my family, though." I lifted my chin. "It has to be the two of you. You are the vessels that will contain Macha's magic."

The mattress sank beside me, and I felt Mom's hands glide over my hair. "Honey, it's all right. If this is what Aster and I are meant to do, it must be for a good reason. The Goddess has never led us astray."

Sybil joined us, sharing in our pain and offering herself up as part of the solution. "Camellia, let me do this instead. I may not be a citizen of the fairy realm, but I am a fully-human witch."

"No," Mom whispered. "It has to be Aster and me. Besides, your coven needs you. And we need you to keep watch over the portals back home.," Mom took Sybil's hand and gave it a light squeeze. "You know as well as I do, when it comes to the Goddess's plan, we all have our parts to play. This is what Aster and I are meant to do," she reiterated.

"What is it that we're meant to do?" Aster's voice floated into the tent, her eyes and concern falling directly on me.

Thankfully, Mom relayed the Goddess's plan and provided Aster the comfort she needed—something I currently wasn't capable of.

This may be the Goddess's plan, but I was still riddled with guilt. "I'm sorry," I apologized again, and excused myself from the tent. Alder sent a wave of love down our bond but remained with Craven inside, giving me as much space and time to process as he could.

Gretta tiptoed across the freshly fallen snow to continually fetch water and snacks for us all—her own way of helping the group. Iris and Fern joined everyone inside a few minutes later and were brought up to speed, while I stood out in the cold, freezing and listening. Finally, after enough self-punishment, I returned to the group and spent hours debating and strategizing until we solidified a plan.

"This is going to work." Mom bobbed her head, and my heart sank all over again.

Lily

Plumes of frosted air escaped my mouth and nose as we tied up the horses in the forest outside the hidden entrance to Craven's mountain. Aster, Mom, and the leader of the Dark Elves would be the only ones to enter the stronghold, while the rest of us waited in the royal tent hidden outside.

General Niasin stationed his men around us so they were spread out in clusters, barely visible through the trees.

"Are you ready?" Mom asked Aster, the crisp mountain air turning her nose pink. My sister nodded and they clasped hands, then Mom turned to me. "Monitor your sister's bond, and as soon as you feel Daisy free again, you'll know it's safe to come inside."

I stepped forward and hugged them both, offering the only advice I could think of. "Please be safe. If for any reason the poultice doesn't work, get out of there as fast as you can."

They both nodded, resolved to the plan, and followed Craven inside the hidden entrance of his mountain stronghold.

Alder came up behind me and wrapped me in his arms. "Everything will be okay. Have faith in your Goddess, my love. Her plan will work."

I truly hope so, or everything will be lost.

Back inside the tent, Fern and Iris sat quietly at the table across the room, while Gretta and Sybil occupied themselves by cleaning every available surface, stoking the fire, and preparing a pot of hearty soup and tea.

"Here, Your Majesty, drink this." Gretta handed me a cup of the same frothy liquid she'd offered me on the trail, and just like before, it warmed me to my core."

"Thank you, my friend. What kind of magical brew is this?" I teased, not expecting an answer back.

"It's a traditional tea from my original homeland, made with herbs and snow. It was carried into battle to help keep our soldiers warm." Gretta pulled a chair close to the fire and sat down, shifting in a way that demanded our attention.

Alder and I sat on the end of the bed with bated breath, waiting to hear her origin story.

"My family ruled the Northern most part of this realm for centuries, beyond even Glenmiere, to a land that no longer exists. Our entire region and ancestral line were wiped from the map during Macha's last cycle as the Crone." Gretta lifted her arm, and a cloud of white frozen mist formed in the palm of her hand. "We can manipulate water, but mostly in the form of ice and mist." She released the bright cloud, letting it splash onto her delicate white shoes.

"It was you who put out the fire in the library that day, wasn't it?" I questioned. "You saved me."

Gretta nodded, confirming my suspicions. "I watched as one queen was lost to this realm, and I couldn't bear to lose another." She reached for my hand. "You're far too important, my dear, and it was time I revealed my secret." Standing from her chair, she took a step to the side and raised her hands in the air. A white light filled the tent, then dissolved like a cotton-candy cloud to reveal Gretta transformed.

Long silver-white braids hung past her waist, and her eyes sparkled a vibrant icy-blue. "My name is Gretta Vorien, Queen of the Ice Fae, and I will forever be at your service."

Twenty-Nine

Aster

After spending the night whispering and discussing our concerns beneath the covers in a single, albeit large tent filled with my family, Craven held my hand and guided me into the depths of his home. Macha may be her strongest here, but so was my fiancé. And because of the deal his ancestors made, she couldn't harm the Dark Elves—a caveat I was most grateful for.

"Since the hidden entrance leads into the dungeons, it will be a bit of a jaunt to reach the throne room." Craven's whisper echoed off the honed-out walls of the cavernous cave. "I can only assume that's where they'll be." He squeezed my hand, and I returned the gesture, grateful to have him with me.

I never expected to find someone in this life. Especially after everything that happened with Lily.

I was a simple human witch. Tasked with protecting our portal, I suddenly found myself the guardian of so much more. Sister to the rightful Fae Queen, at fifteen, I became utterly unimportant overnight—not that I minded. I was so proud of Lily. But burying my nose in a book to study and learn was my preferred escape, and after all those years of keeping that secret, Lily learned the truth and claimed her throne, leaving me to aid my family the best way I could with the only skill set I had. In doing so, I retreated further into myself, my usual stoic demeanor becoming even more rigid and cold.

Within my own struggles, I pushed everyone too far. I pushed them all away, but I couldn't help it. I was unable to find the balance within myself to maintain our sisterly bond—especially after their fae magic was released and a true bond between them was formed. I was surrounded by spectacular women and became an even harder version of myself.

Resigned to the Ferindale castle, I spent most of my days training my sisters to harness their new elemental powers and my nights hiding in the shadows of any empty room I could find.

That's where Craven found me. Where Craven saw me for who I was and embraced me, hard edges and all.

That's where Craven and I fell in love… in the shadows.

"Almost there." His husky voice sent a shiver down my spine, and I reached back for Mom's hand.

This was it. We'd be facing the Fae Goddess of Death as two human witches, and I could only pray that Lily's vision was accurate and our plan would work.

At the top of the stone steps, Craven pushed open a thick slab door, and we emerged from the prison cavern and into the main hall. Mom and I retained our silence, but I could feel her mind and eyes roaming over the massive pillars and sparkling floor of the Dark Elves' stronghold, the same as mine. The interior of the mountain walls shimmered here as well, blanketed in a soft, sparkling glow, though due to Macha's presence, it too seemed muted and dimmer than it should have been. Intricate carvings of animals and trees were etched deep into the stone of the ceilings and walls, and I smiled at the cold, yet thoughtful precision of the palace that I would soon call home.

"This way." Craven guided us away from the main hall to another set of stairs carved into the side of the mountain. We dropped each other's hands and silently marched upward, tiptoeing toward the massive wood door at the top of the landing.

I could hear Daisy's voice inside, but it, too, carried a taint. The wrongness of it rubbed against my skin, making me want to dig in my nails and scratch it away until I bled. Mom reached for my hand again.

Craven nodded to us both, then leaned in and gave me a kiss. "I love you, Aster. And as I've already told you, that won't change regardless of what happens here."

I had no time to process the emotions his affection elicited as the thick door swung open, revealing Daisy and Bennett inside.

"We've been expecting you," Daisy drawled, "but I admit, I thought I'd be seeing the King and Queen."

Craven, Mom, and I slowly eased our way inside, keeping our backs to the wall and staying near the door.

Bennett shut the heavy wooden barrier with a click, then twisted the brass lock, trapping us inside.

"Honey, I'm so glad you're... *okay*," Mom started, but was cut off by Daisy's vicious laugh.

I cringed at the sound. This was no longer the sister I knew, and whatever she'd become was definitely *not* okay.

"Thank you for your concern, Mother. Bennett and I are very happy with how things have turned out."

It couldn't be true, and I waited for Mom to ease into a gentle conversation, keeping things light and civil as Craven and I edged closer to Bennett with the poultice in hand. But instead—

"Really? You're *happy* with how things have turned out?" Mom snapped, rage bolstering her words. "Infected with dark magic and destroying every beautiful part of this land? Tainting the creatures of the realm to do your bidding? Attacking your own family!!! *That's* what makes you happy?" Mom yelled.

Daisy flinched, as if a small part of her were still there and recognized the truth in Mom's words, and when Bennett reached out to comfort her, Craven and I made our move.

Craven lunged toward Bennett, pulling him back against his barrel chest with his staff holding him in place. I raced to smear the Fairy Triad poultice across Bennett's exposed skin and gasped when the result was instantaneous. Black smoke rose from Bennett's pores, gathering in the air as if looking for a new place to land.

Mom took advantage of the shocked lull in the room and smeared her poultice down Daisy's outstretched arm.

Daisy screamed and dropped to the floor—her reaction much more violent than Bennett's, and there was nothing we could do but watch. She convulsed and writhed on the floor while the Fairy Triad sank into her skin, forcing out Macha's black magic in a powerful, gushing stream.

Daisy and Bennett's darkness gathered before us, coalesced, and quickly took on a form of its own. The Goddess was being pulled into existence, and now was our chance.

Craven gathered and watched over Bennett and Daisy in the corner of the room, while Mom and I stepped forward, prepared for what we had to do.

Holding hands, we called on our magic and opened ourselves up to the spell we were about to cast. With one last look over my shoulder, I smiled at Craven and prayed he'd still love me after I accepted the darkness of a Death Goddess inside.

My voice joined Mom's as we called out the chant.

"Ties that bind, darkness entwined.
Settle here, in body not mind.
Free from your cycle shall you be.
Contained in flesh, so mote it be."

It was a simple combination of the two spells we used before, and when Macha's darkness drifted toward us, I knew that it had worked.

Thirty

Lily

Dark clouds gathered above the Dark Elf stronghold, blanketing the entire area in a storm of lightning and stone. Sizzling energy cracked again and again, sending debris from the mountainside crashing down atop our tent.

"We have to get inside the mountain," Alder shouted into the chaos, waving an arm to dismiss General Niasin and his men from the trees beyond.

Iris, Fern, Gretta, and I followed Alder through the hidden crack in the side of the stone, completely drenched as we emerged inside.

"I assume this means your plan worked." Alder raised a brow in my direction.

"Or that it didn't, and Macha is fighting back." Gretta's assumption matched my own, but I wouldn't allow myself to fall into fear.

"Only one way to find out." I nodded toward the door at the top of the steep stone stairs, floors above where we currently stood.

Looking below us into the cavernous depths of the Dark Elf prison, Fern shuddered beside me, almost dropping to her knees.

Oh, no. I hadn't thought about how being back here again would affect her. *"Fern, I'm so sorry. Are you okay? Do you want to wait outside?"* I sent my apology and lame suggestion down the bond between us, layered with genuine concern.

Iris extended a hand, steadying her twin on her feet. "We've got this."

She nudged Fern's shoulder, earning a tearful smile from Fern and myself.

"Okay," I nodded, "let's go."

Up and up we climbed, nary a word between us. The storm raged outside, sending echoes of falling rocks reverberating off the mountain's inner core. The deep thrum of them crashing against the stone created a bone-rattling beat as if we were caught inside a massive, hollow drum. And I guess in a way we were.

Finally gathered at the landing, most of us bent over at the waist and struggled to catch our breath.

"Everyone stay behind me," Alder instructed, and we all nodded our agreement.

Creeping into the Dark Elf stronghold felt strange, knowing it would soon be home to our sister and friend. And when screams echoed off the walls from an unseen room above, *strange* was definitely the word to describe the feeling coursing through my veins.

It sounded like Daisy, but when I reached out for her through our bond, there was still no response. I looked up to Alder, mentally sharing my concern, and we immediately picked up our pace.

Racing up the stairs to the throne room, we found the thick wooden door thrown open wide, and we all eased inside.

Craven, Bennett, and Daisy stood huddled in the corner, and I suddenly realized it was Aster who was screaming as Mom lay passed out on the floor.

"No! This can't be happening!" Aster yelled, dropping to her knees.

I rushed to meet her, falling to the floor beside her and Mom. "Aster, what happened? What's wrong? Did the spell not work?"

My sister frantically ran her hands up and down Mom's body, hovering barely an inch above her skin.

"Help me! Use your magic to pull it out of her!" Aster's eyes were wild, darting around the room filled with a fear I didn't recognize.

I laid a hand on her arm, but she jerked away. "Aster, please. You must tell me what happened first. I can't help you unless I know."

Her arms fell limply to her sides, and she hung her head, the words floating from her lips in a ghostly whisper. "All of Macha's dark magic went into Mom, and none into me." She raised her head and tears ran down her cheeks. "She is full of the crone's death magic now, and I'm afraid it's too much for one person to bear. We have to save her."

Lily

Gutted by the information, we all moved at a snail's pace, as if restrained by the Goddess's death magic as well. Step by step, Craven gingerly carried Mom down to the large meeting room on the main floor, laying her on the same cot Fern had occupied only a few months ago.

"Can we just perform the spell again?" Daisy asked, fully recovered. "Use the poultice to pull it out of her, then alter the wording to make sure it's split between the two of them instead?"

With our bond repaired, I felt the guilt and sadness she now carried within—and her desperation to set things right. "Lil, did you hear me?" Daisy pressed.

"I heard you, but I don't know if it will work. Releasing Macha's magic again may be the worst thing we could possibly do. What if it infects you again? Or Fern, or Iris?" *Or Alder, or me,* I thought selfishly.

"We have to try something!" Daisy threw up her hands and melted into Bennett's arms, guilt and fear clearly riding them both.

"This isn't your fault, you know? Either of you." I shared my statement out loud to make sure everyone knew I didn't blame them and could only hope they felt the same.

Bennett bowed his head, and a warmth radiated amongst us four sisters. I smiled, grateful to have back even a sliver of normalcy during this difficult time. We'd always been able to count on each other, sharing our magic when needed, and now was no different. In fact…

"I have an idea," I announced to the room.

I stared down at Mom, noting for the first time ever how small and delicate she was. To me, she had always been this powerful witch, a force to be reckoned with. A woman strong enough to raise five daughters by herself. She was a hero to us all. But now, staring at her frail form, I could only hope she was strong enough to survive this.

Everyone gathered around the large stone table, waiting to hear my new plan.

"I believe we've been given these new powers for a reason. The prophecy Gideon shared with Mom said these were the elemental powers of our fae ancestors, and I think they have something to do with all of this." I waved an arm around the room. "What's happening now has happened before, but there was no one present to wield all the elements at once." I took a moment to look everyone in the eye and felt the rightness of my words all the way to my soul. "I believe us working together is the key to stopping Macha once and for all."

Thirty-One

Lily

"Our end goal remains the same. Macha's magic must be divided between Aster and Mom to keep the Goddess from moving through her phases again. But this time, we'll use our elemental powers to make sure she doesn't have a chance to infect someone else or escape before we can recast the spell." I nodded to each of my sisters and Gretta as we stood together next to Mom's cot.

Sybil, Alder, Craven, and Bennett spread themselves out by the door—a barrier of brain and brawn should Macha's essence escape us.

I lifted my hand, and Gretta began, encasing Mom beneath a thin mist of ice. Aster leaned down and swiped a handful of the remaining poultice across Mom's chest, and we all braced for what we expected to happen next.

Right on queue, tendrils of thick black smoke rose from Mom's skin, swirling and hovering beneath Gretta's layer of ice like a snake trapped inside a balloon.

Poking and prodding the surface, Macha's energy began to slam against the ice, bouncing back and forth between the barrier and Mom's skin.

"Shit! If it can't get out, it's going to go right back into Mom," Daisy shouted, and I had no reason to doubt her. Out of everyone, she knew best what the Goddess of Death would do.

"Let it out," I instructed Gretta as I created a fire ball in the palm of my hand.

My sisters followed suit, each gathering their elemental magic in weapon form.

Iris held a crystal knife that could tear through any enemy, while Fern solidified her water into sharp barbs of ice as well. Daisy's hands were turned upright at her sides, each holding a mini tornado that she could enlarge at a moment's notice, and Gretta now held a warriors spear made entirely of ice.

Gretta released her mist, and Macha's dark energy exploded into the room, knocking us all to the ground.

"Stop it! Freeze it again!" Aster shouted as we all unleashed our gifts.

But none of them met their mark.

Overpowered by the sheer vastness of the Goddess's magic, we all watched in horror as it blew past the others and disappeared out the door.

Racing into the corridor, we searched high and low.

"There!" Craven shouted, spotting the slinking tail of Macha's magic as it burrowed beneath the carved stairs that led to the upper floors.

Inching cautiously forward, we all stepped into the shadows and gathered around the gaping hole now present in the solid stone wall.

"What should we do now?" Fern asked, poised with her ice daggers at the ready.

"I'm not sure. Maybe I could burn it out?" I lifted my hand, illuminating the hole with a fire ball and gasped when it suddenly sealed shut.

Shit!

"What the hell?" Daisy shouted and tossed a blast of air against the wall.

The rest of us joined in, hammering the sealed-over stone with our elemental gifts until the mountain itself shuddered around us.

Thunder crashed outside, echoing deep throughout the mountain again. Conditions were deteriorating fast, and it was no longer safe to remain inside. We'd lost control, and everything was happening too fast.

Craven guided us to the front door, a thick barricade of carved wood, steel, and stone that stood at least twelve feet high.

Pushing it open with the palm of his hand, the leader of the Dark Elves peered outside and cursed. "Damn. And here I thought we might actually win." Black clouds blanketed the entire sky, flashing wildly with murderous intent. "Instead, it seems I now have a Death Goddess residing in the belly of my mountain, like a crazed dragon guarding her hoard."

Aster sank into Craven's embrace, and I did the same with Alder. Daisy found her way into Bennett's arms, and Mom gathered the rest of our sisters and friends into a group hug.

Soaked and defeated, we trudged our way to the edge of the forest where our tent and horses remained. Looking back to the Dark Elf stronghold, guilt rendered me speechless.

The top of Craven's mountain was covered in a layer of dark magic, seeping down its sides and turning everything to dust. Evergreens snapped and wilted before our eyes, and in the distance, pops of red sizzled into the air as the magical vilenflu flowers were destroyed once again.

The combined sobs of my family filtered through the forest, and a deep-seated rage took root in my chest. "This cannot stand! We are not losing our home again!" Pulled by an instinctive thread, I reached for the essence of my Fae magic and willed it to gather in physical form.

My husband, family, and dear friends gasped as a flaming crown flared to life above my head.

As the true Fae Queen of this realm, I was physically and spiritually tied to this land, and I would do whatever I must to protect every inch. Remembering the image of the elaborate tree, full and blooming with life while cocooning a woman's body in its twisted roots, I took a deep breath and let the crown atop my head flare until my entire body was covered in white hot flames.

With a final look to Alder, I repeated the phrase from Gwenlyth's book of shadows and sank beneath the ground, burning my way to the very core of our world. "From essence to embers, and embers to dust. A Queen will *always* do as she must."

The end… for now!

Continue reading for Lily and Alder's next adventure…

THE ELF HANDBOOK TO STORMS AND STONE

(Book 4 in the Stolen Spells series)

by

Tish Thawer

One

Lily

An orange glow surrounded me, blinding me to the dangers outside. Thunder rumbled in my ears, and I couldn't remember why I was here.

"Come on, silly. Get your head out from under that umbrella and join the fun." Daisy waved me over to where our other two sisters were stomping through every pot-hole and puddle that lined our street.

Ah, yes! They convinced me to go out in the storm to watch for the rainbows that would inevitably form after the rain. Now, I remembered.

"We can still see the rainbows from inside the shop, you know? Why do you always force me out into this mess." I yanked my raincoat tighter and crouched beneath my umbrella's protective dome.

"Because… this is part of the fun," Fern teased, splashing me with a kick of her boot.

"I think what you and I consider fun, are two very different things." I smiled but couldn't resist splashing her back.

"Girls, it's time to come inside," Mom called out from our shop's purple front door, and we all raced to the back of the house.

Shaking off the rain, we deposited our gear in the mud room and ran upstairs, magically dry by the time we reached the living room rug.

Aster was there, of course, sitting beside the fire with her nose buried in a book. "What are you reading about this time?" I asked.

My oldest sister removed her tortoiseshell glasses and smiled up at me with her bright hazel eyes. "It's a story about a fairy queen, and how she saved her entire world with the help of her family and friends."

I flopped down in front of her, crossed my legs, and rested my chin on my fists. "That sounds like an amazing story. Tell me more."

Acknowledgments

To my husband: Thank you for all the sacrifices *you* make.

To my children: I support you. Love you. And am proud to be your mom.

To Molly Phipps: Thank you for another beautiful design to bring this series together as a whole.

To my editor, Kristie Cook of Ang'dora Productions: Thank you for the last-minute assist and your amazing guidance. This book wouldn't be as good without you, my friend.

To Cortney, Sharon, and all my beta readers: Thank you for reading *TQHEE* before publication and providing your feedback and editorial reviews. I'm so grateful to have such amazing friends in this industry. You are all the best!

And finally, to my readers, old and new: As always, thank you for following me down the primrose path and into another adventure. I can't wait to embark on our next one together! Your continued support means the world to me.

About the Author

#1 Bestseller in Historical Fiction
Top 100 Bestselling in Paid Kindle Store
Best Cover Award Winner
Readers' Choice Award Winner
Best Sci-fi Fantasy Novel Winner (x2)

Author Tish Thawer writes young adult fantasy and paranormal fiction for all ages. From her first paranormal cartoon, *Isis*, to the *Twilight* phenomenon, myth, magic, and superpowers have always held a special place in her heart. Best known for her *Witches of BlackBrook* series, Tish's detailed world-building and magic-laced stories have been compared to Nora Roberts, Sam Cheever, and Charlaine Harris. Tish's books have been featured in *British Glamour* and *Elle* magazines. Tish has worked as a computer consultant, photographer, and graphic designer and has bylines as a columnist for Gliterary Girl media, *RT* magazine, and *Literary Lunes* magazine. She currently resides in Missouri with her husband and three wonderful children, and operates Amber Leaf Designs, an online custom swag retail store, and Amber Leaf Farms, a lavender and flower farm that opened in 2022.

You can find out more about Tish and all her titles by visiting: www.tishthawer.com

Connect with Tish Thawer Online:
Instagram: @tishthawer
Facebook: www.facebook.com/AuthorTishThawer
Twitter: @tishthawer
Pinterest: www.pinterest.com/tishthawer/

If you'd like an email when each new book releases, please sign up for my mailing list. Emails only go out about once per month and your information is closely guarded.
http://www.tishthawer.com/subscribe.html

Also, to get an email for new releases, book updates, and special sales, follow me on BookBub and Goodreads at the links below:
www.bookbub.com/authors/tish-thawer
https://www.goodreads.com/tishthawer

Again, thank you for reading. If you'd like to stay connected and hang out for more magical adventures, you can join my private reader group here:
https://www.facebook.com/groups/TishThawersBookCoven

Blessed be,
~ Tish

Also by Tish Thawer

Stolen Spells
The Witch Handbook to Magic and Mayhem – Book 1
The Fairy Handbook to Spells and Salvation – Book 2
The Queen's Handbook to Essence and Embers – Book 3
The Elf Handbook to Storms and Stone – Book 4

The Witches of BlackBrook
The Witches of BlackBrook - Book 1
The Daughters of Maine - Book 2
The Sisters of Salem – Book 3
Lost in Time – (A Legends of Havenwood Falls novella, and a Witches of BlackBrook side-story)

The Women of Purgatory
Raven's Breath - Book 1
Dark Abigail - Book 2
Holli's Hellfire – Book 3
The Women of Purgatory: The Complete Series bundle

The TS901 Chronicles
TS901: Anomaly – Book 1
TS901: Dominion – Book 2
TS901: Evolution – Book 3
The TS901 Chronicles – Complete Set

Havenwood Falls Shared World
Lost in Time – (A Legends of Havenwood Falls novella, and a Witches of BlackBrook side-story)
Sun & Moon Academy – Book 1: Fall Semester
Sun & Moon Academy – Book 2: Spring Semester
Havenwood Falls Sunset Anthology

Also by Tish Thawer cont'd

The Rose Trilogy
Scent of a White Rose - Book 1
Roses & Thorns - Book 1.5
Blood of a Red Rose - Book 2
Death of a Black Rose - Book 3
The Rose Trilogy – 10th Anniversary Edition

The Ovialell Series
Aradia Awakens - Book 1
Dark Seeds - Novella (Book 1.5)
Prophecy's Child - Companion
The Rise of Rae - Companion
Shay and the Box of Nye - Companion
Behind the Veil - Omnibus

Stand-Alones
Weaver
Guiding Gaia
Handler
Moon Kissed
Dance With Me
Magical Journal & Planner (non-fiction)
Found & Foraged (non-fiction)

Anthologies
The Monster Ball: Year 3
Fairy Tale Confessions
Losing It: A Collection of V-Cards
Christmas Lites II

For another adventure,

please enjoy this excerpt from

Raven's Breath

Book 1 in The Women of Purgatory series

Will she be your Grim Reaper or your Saving Grace?

Raven can breathe life into you, or siphon the life from you...the choice is yours.

They say your life flashes before your eyes when you die. But what you didn't know...your last thoughts determine whether Raven becomes your grim reaper or your saving grace.

Death has a sinister plan, but his favorite female reaper has been given a new power that will combat his secret mission. The only issue...she hasn't discovered it yet.

Will Raven put the pieces together in time, or will Purgatory be destroyed forever?

1

Sirens blared, cutting through the still night, while I watched from the shadows. A man who'd just been hit by a taxi lay bleeding on the frigid, grime covered ground. People began to gather and were staring at the gruesome scene, while the driver of the taxi sat on the curb, crying into his hands.

I scanned the crowd, singling out who'd seen death before and who hadn't.

I could always tell.

My attention snapped back to the dying man when he took his last breath. Images began to take shape in his mind; images that due to my *job*, I, too, could see.

Snapshots of him riding a motorcycle for the first time, of him falling in love, of his big successful promotion at work...all images of him. It was the usual replay of one's life flashing before his eyes.

When the replay stopped, it was time for me to go to work.

I stepped out of the shadows and took two steps in his direction. To the people watching, his wide eyes marked his final passing, but to me they continued to grow as he took in my features: dark hair blowing in the wind, a curvaceous body wrapped in tight black leather, and large wings the color of the night sky. No one could see me but him, for he now resided in the netherworld...in my world.

I extended my hand and offered my usual greeting. "My name is Raven, and I'm here to help you find peace." He reached for me, then glanced back to take a final look at his body.

"Am I really dead?"

"Yes."

"And you are..."

"The Grim Reaper."

This was the exact conversation I'd had with thousands of souls, which was why I knew that *now* would be the best time to comfort him, before he got scared to death—no pun intended—and tried to flee from me.

I extended my wings and let my divine light radiate from within. "There's nothing to fear."

This usually worked since I looked more like an angel with wings than the old man with a scythe that most people envisioned. Maybe that's why I'd been chosen to become the first female Reaper in history; the boys had been losing too many souls.

My inner light built to its crescendo, opening the portal to Heaven. It was through a Reaper's inner light that all souls were transported to their destined eternity, whether it be Heaven or Hell.

I guided the man to the pearly gates, then quickly returned the same way to the earthly plane and flew to the highest point of the Holy Cross Cemetery. It was the oldest and largest in the "city of cemeteries," Colma, California, located just south of San Francisco. I tucked my wings into my back and walked up the hill, the heels of my boots sinking into the dirt that surrounded the large mausoleum.

The name over the ornate stone entrance read Richard Payman, Born 1892 - Died 1962. I placed my hand on the door's handle and the letters R. and P. became illuminated. I smiled when the numbers shifted and transformed into the sum of their total—1+8+9+2+1+9+6+2, equaling 38. In other words...**R**eaper **P**ortal, Thirty-eight.

There were thousands of portals, each one located in a cemetery tomb that read Richard Payman, Born "something" – Died "something else," to indicate which location you were entering.

The seam of the door glowed blue, then opened to reveal the shimmering orb waiting within. If a human opened this door, however, all they would see was a stone sarcophagus holding *Mr. Payman's* remains.

The portals were the only entrance to our world; the world of Death and his Reapers, a.k.a. Purgatory.

I stepped through and the city greeted me. A wide expanse of dark stone buildings and gothic turrets dotted the light gray sky. Inky tendrils swirled and floated through the air, extending as far as the eye could see.

The black smoke-like wisps were the souls that refused to move on—the phenoms.

Whenever a soul tried to flee, they would instead "stick" to the Reapers until we returned to Purgatory, where they were sucked into the sky to wander aimlessly for all eternity.

Poor bastards.

I flew towards the main building, hoping to check-in and be done before I started my long weekend. I touched down on the slate steps and took a moment to compose myself before entering the massive castle.

At present, I was the only female Reaper in Death's employ, but according to rumors, I wasn't sure how long that would be the case. It didn't surprise me; I'd been a huge help in lowering the numbers of lost souls, but to be honest, I wasn't sure if I wanted to share the title of *"one and only."*

"Good evening, Raven." My eyes shifted. Death's long bony fingers wrapped a staccato beat against the round heads that made up the armrests of his creepy skull throne. "How are you?"

All Reapers worked for Death, but I doubted anyone in Purgatory actually liked being in his presence. Then again...maybe it was just me.

"I'm great, thank you. I was just checking-in before I headed home."

A smile played on his lips. "While I always enjoy seeing you, you shouldn't feel obligated to check-in with me. Your numbers are consistent and you haven't let me down yet."

His words carried an edge that left me worried I'd somehow done exactly that. I swallowed hard against the lump in my throat, nodded and turned away.

"Raven, a quick question before you leave?" Death asked, polite as always.

A slow breath escaped my lips. *So much for a speedy escape.* I turned around slowly and plastered a smile on my face.

"Sure. What's up?"

"I've been thinking about bringing on another female Reaper––since you've proven to be such a valuable asset," he added. His leer made my skin crawl. "But I wanted to talk to you first, of course, before I made my final decision and see what you thought of the idea."

Ha! Like he gave a damn what I thought. He'd do whatever he wanted, and I knew without a doubt this was just his way of watching me squirm.

I tossed my hair over my shoulder and smiled. "Actually, I think that's a great idea. I've been playing clean up for so long, it might be nice to have a little help around here."

Hmph. I don't squirm.

For another adventure,
please enjoy this **early** excerpt from
For the Love of Penelope Green

Worlds apart, the memory of Penelope Green haunts Graham until his dying days. But in a realm of eternal Gods, death only means another assignment to prove your worth.

Tasked with maintaining the divine garden, Graham Daniels utilizes his horticultural skills in hopes of creating something so hauntingly beautiful even the Gods will take note. More importantly, he longs for Penelope to notice his creation back on Earth and remember the love they shared.

As above, so below, entwined like roots, our love still grows.

With *For the Love of Penelope Green*, Tish Thawer delivers a sweeping fantasy romance that spans heaven and earth, with the touch of magic that's rooted in the unbreakable bond of love.

One

Penelope

My dearest GD,

The day I lost you was the worst and best day of my life. The worst for obvious reasons. The loss. The pain. The grief. Losing the only person I had ever loved broke me in unexpected ways. But it was also the best, because it gave me hope. Hope and the courage to no longer fear death. For now I know there is something to look forward to—being reunited with you. That thought alone is the beacon that guides me in the dead of night. Once my time comes, I look forward to joining you in the land of the Gods. Until then, I'll focus all my love into the beauty we created together here on Earth. I'll tend to our garden with reverence and care, and bury my words beneath its soil, hoping the Gods allow you to receive them.

With all the love in both our words—Yours forever, PG

***

Graham

The familiar ring in my head brought me to my knees in the dirt. Digging until my nails were full of soil, I finally found it—Penelope's next letter.

Wiping away the remaining speckles of earth, I stared at her initials on the damp piece of parchment in my hand. I had no idea what first made her bury her letters in the soil of our garden back home, but I was so very grateful she did.

By the grace of the Gods, I was able to retrieve them here in the divine garden—my heavenly occupation and where I'd spent all my days since passing on.

Unfolding the letter, I read it twice before tucking it into my shirt pocket, grateful to keep it to myself. Grateful for the hope it gave me. Having something tangible to hold onto until we could be together again was a blessing. One I vowed to keep secret, or risk losing forever.

Coming in 2025

www.ingramcontent.com/pod-product-compliance
Lightning Source LLC
LaVergne TN
LVHW042251070526
838201LV00110B/332/J